A FINE WILL BE CHARGED
FOR EACH OVERDUE BOOK

D1127872

Mr. MUNCHAUSEN

Yours for truth
Baron Munchausen

MR. MUNCHAUSEN

Being a TRUE ACCOUNT *of some of the* RECENT AD-
VENTURES *beyond the* STYX *of the late* HIERONYMUS
CARL FRIEDRICH, *sometime* BARON MUNCHAUSEN *of*
BODENWERDER, *as originally reported for the* SUNDAY EDI-
TION *of the* GEHENNA GAZETTE *by its* SPECIAL IN-
TERVIEWER *the late* Mr. ANANIAS *formerly of* JERUSALEM
and now first transcribed from the columns of that JOURNAL *by*

JOHN KENDRICK BANGS
Embellished with Drawings by
PETER NEWELL

Short Story Index Reprint Series

BOOKS FOR LIBRARIES PRESS
FREEPORT, NEW YORK

First Published 1901
Reprinted 1969

STANDARD BOOK NUMBER:
8369-3013-4

LIBRARY OF CONGRESS CATALOG CARD NUMBER:
78-81261

EDITOR'S APOLOGY

and

DEDICATION

IN order that there may be no misunderstanding as to the why and the wherefore of this collection of tales it appears to me to be desirable that I should at the outset state my reasons for acting as the medium between the spirit of the late Baron Munchausen and the reading public. In common with a large number of other great men in history Baron Munchausen has suffered because he is not understood. I have observed with wondering surprise the steady and constant growth of the idea that Baron Munchausen was not a man of truth; that his statements of fact were untrustworthy, and that as a realist he had no standing whatsoever. Just how this misconception of the man's character has arisen it would be difficult to say. Surely in his published writings he shows that same lofty resolve to be true to life as he has seen it that characterises the work of some of the high Apostles of Realism, who are writing of the things that will *teach future generations how we of to-day ordered our goings-on. The note of veracity in Baron Munchausen's early literary venturings rings as clear and as true certainly as the similar note in the charming studies of Manx Realism that have come to us of late years from the pen of Mr. Corridor Walkingstick, of Gloomster Abbey and London. We all remember the glow of satisfaction with which we read Mr. Walkingstick's great story of the love of the clergyman, John Stress, for the charming little heroine, Glory Partridge. Here was something at last that rang true. The picture was painted in the boldest of colours, and, regardless of consequences to himself, Mr. Walkingstick dared to be real when he might have given rein to his imagination. Mr. Walkingstick was, thereupon, lifted up by popular favour to the level of an apostle—nay, he even admitted the soft impeachment—and now as a moral teacher he is without a rival in the world of literature. Yet the same age that accepts this man as a moral teacher, rejects Baron Munchausen, who, in different manner perhaps, presented to the world as true and life-like a picture of the conditions of*

EDITOR'S APOLOGY *and* DEDICATION

his day as that given to us by Mr. Walkingstick in his deservedly popular romance, " Episcopalians I have Met." Of course, I do not claim that Baron Munchausen's stories in bulk or in specified instances, have the literary vigour that is so marked a quality of the latter-day writer, but the point I do wish to urge is that to accept the one as a veracious chronicler of his time and to reject the other as one who indulges his pen in all sorts of grotesque vagaries, without proper regard for the facts, is a great injustice to the man of other times. The question arises, why is this? How has this wrong upon the worthy realist of the eighteenth century been perpetrated? Is it an intentional or an unwitting wrong? I prefer to believe that it is based upon ignorance of the Baron's true quality, due to the fact that his works are rarely to be found within the reach of the public: in some cases, because of the failure of librarians to comprehend his real motives, his narratives are excluded from Public and Sunday-School libraries; and because of their extreme age, they are not easily again brought into vogue. I have, therefore, accepted the office of in-

ix

termediary between the Baron and the readers of the present day, in order that his later work, which, while it shows to a marked degree the decadence of his literary powers, may yet serve to demonstrate to the readers of my own time how favourably he compares with some of the literary idols of to-day, in the simple matter of fidelity to fact. If these stories which follow shall serve to rehabilitate Baron Munchausen as a lover and practitioner of the arts of Truth, I shall not have made the sacrifice of my time in vain. If they fail of this purpose I shall still have the satisfaction of knowing that I have tried to render a service to an honest and defenceless man.

Meanwhile I dedicate this volume, with sentiments of the highest regard, to that other great realist

MR. CORRIDOR WALKINGSTICK

of

GLOOMSTER ABBEY

J. K. B.

Contents

List of Illustrations

LIST *of* ILLUSTRATIONS

Mr. MUNCHAUSEN

An Account of His
Recent Adventures

MR. MUNCHAUSEN

I

I ENCOUNTER THE OLD GENTLEMAN

THERE are moments of supreme embarrass-
ment in the lives of persons given to veracity,
—indeed it has been my own unusual experience in life that the truth well stuck to is twice as
hard a proposition as a lie so obvious that no one is
deceived by it at the outset. I cannot quite agree
with my friend, Caddy Barlow, who says that in a
tight place it is better to lie at once and be done
with it than to tell the truth which will need forty
more truths to explain it, but I must confess that in
my forty years of absolute and conscientious devo-
tion to truth I have found myself in holes far
deeper than any my most mendacious of friends
ever got into. I do not propose, however, to desert
at this late hour the Goddess I have always wor-
shipped because she leads me over a rough and
rocky road, and whatever may be the hardships
involved in my wooing I intend to the very end to

3

remain the ever faithful slave of Mademoiselle Veracité. All of which I state here in prefatory mood, and in order, in so far as it is possible for me to do so, to disarm the incredulous and sniffy reader who may be inclined to doubt the truth of my story of how the manuscript of the following pages came into my possession. I am quite aware that to some the tale will appear absolutely and intolerably impossible. I know that if any other than I told it to me I should not believe it. Yet despite these drawbacks the story is in all particulars, essential and otherwise, absolutely truthful.

The facts are briefly these:

It was not, to begin with, a dark and dismal evening. The snow was not falling silently, clothing a sad and gloomy world in a mantle of white, and over the darkling moor a heavy mist was not rising, as is so frequently the case. There was no soul-stirring moaning of bitter winds through the leafless boughs; so far as I was aware nothing soughed within twenty miles of my bailiwick; and my dog, lying before a blazing log fire in my library, did not give forth an occasional growl of ap-

4

prehension, denoting the presence or approach of an uncanny visitor from other and mysterious realms: and for two good reasons. The first reason is that it was midsummer when the thing happened, so that a blazing log fire in my library would have been an extravagance as well as an anachronism. The second is that I have no dog. In fact there was nothing unusual, or uncanny in the whole experience. It happened to be a bright and somewhat too sunny July day, which is not an unusual happening along the banks of the Hudson. You could see the heat, and if anything had soughed it could only have been the mercury in my thermometer. This I must say clicked nervously against the top of the glass tube and manifested an extraordinary desire to climb higher than the length of the tube permitted. Incidentally I may add, even if it be not believed, that the heat was so intense that the mercury actually did raise the whole thermometer a foot and a half above the mantel-shelf, and for two mortal hours, from midday until two by the Monastery Clock, held it suspended there in mid-air with no visible means of support. Not a breath of air was stirring, and the only sounds heard were the expanding creaks of the beams of my house, which upon that particular day increased eight feet in width and assumed a height which made it appear to be a three instead of a two story dwelling. There was little work doing in the house. The children played about in their bathing suits, and the only other active factor in my life of the moment was our hired man who was kept busy in the cellar pouring water on the furnace coal to keep it from spontaneously combusting.

We had just had luncheon, burning our throats with the iced tea and with considerable discomfort swallowing the simmering cold roast filet, which we had to eat hastily before the heat of the day transformed it into smoked beef. My youngest boy Willie perspired so copiously that we seriously thought of sending for a plumber to solder up his pores, and as for myself who have spent three summers of my life in the desert of Sahara in order to rid myself of nervous chills to which I was once unhappily subject, for the first time in my life I was impelled to admit that it was intolerably warm. And then the telephone bell rang.

" Great Scott! " I cried, " Who in thunder do you suppose wants to play golf on a day like this? " —for nowadays our telephone is used for no other purpose than the making or the breaking of golf engagements.

" Me," cried my eldest son, whose grammar is not as yet on a par with his activity. " I'll go."

The boy shot out of the dining room and ran to the telephone, returning in a few moments with the statement that a gentleman with a husky voice whose name was none of his business wished to speak with me on a matter of some importance to myself.

I was loath to go. My friends the book agents had recently acquired the habit of approaching me over the telephone, and I feared that here was another nefarious attempt to foist a thirty-eight volume tabloid edition of *The World's Worst Literature* upon me. Nevertheless I wisely determined to respond.

" Hello," I said, placing my lips against the rub-

7

ber cup. "Hello there, who wants 91162 Nepperhan?"

"Is that you?" came the answering question, and, as my boy had indicated, in a voice whose chief quality was huskiness.

"I guess so," I replied facetiously;—"It was this morning, but the heat has affected me somewhat, and I don't feel as much like myself as I might. What can I do for you?"

"Nothing, but you can do a lot for yourself," was the astonishing answer. "Pretty hot for literary work, isn't it?" the voice added sympathetically.

"Very," said I. "Fact is I can't seem to do anything these days but perspire."

"That's what I thought; and when you can't work ruin stares you in the face, eh? Now I have a manuscript—

"Oh Lord!" I cried. "Don't. There are millions in the same fix. Even my cook writes."

"Don't know about that," he returned instantly. "But I do know that there's millions in my manuscript. And you can have it for the asking. How's that for an offer?"

8

"Very kind, thank you," said I. "What's the nature of your story?"

"It's extremely good-natured," he answered promptly.

I laughed. The twist amused me.

"That isn't what I meant exactly," said I, "though it has some bearing on the situation. Is it a Henry James dandy, or does it bear the mark of Caine? Is it realism or fiction?"

"Realism," said he. "Fiction isn't in my line."

"Well, I'll tell you," I replied; "you send it to me by post and I'll look it over. If I can use it I will."

"Can't do it," said he. "There isn't any post-office where I am."

"What?" I cried. "No post-office? Where in Hades are you?"

"Gehenna," he answered briefly. "The transportation between your country and mine is all one way," he added. "If it wasn't the population here would diminish."

"Then how the deuce am I to get hold of your stuff?" I demanded.

"That's easy. Send your stenographer to the 'phone and I'll dictate it," he answered.

The novelty of the situation appealed to me. Even if my new found acquaintance were some funny person nearer at hand than Gehenna trying to play a practical joke upon me, still it might be worth while to get hold of the story he had to tell. Hence I agreed to his proposal.

"All right, sir," said I. " I'll do it. I'll have him here to-morrow morning at nine o'clock sharp. What's your number? I'll ring you up."

"Never mind that," he replied. " I'm merely a tapster on your wires. I'll ring *you* up as soon as I've had breakfast and then we can get to work."

"Very good," said I. "And may I ask your name?"

"Certainly," he answered. " I'm Munchausen."

"What? The Baron?" I roared, delighted.

"Well—I used to be Baron," he returned with a tinge of sadness in his voice, " but here in Gehenna we are all on an equal footing. I'm plain Mr. Munchausen of Hades now. But that's a detail. Don't forget. Nine o'clock. Good-bye."

10

"Wait a moment, Baron," I cried. "How about the royalties on this book?"

"Keep 'em for yourself," he replied. "We have money to burn over here. You are welcome to all the earthly rights of the book. I'm satisfied with the returns on the Asbestos Edition, already in its 468th thousand. Good-bye."

There was a rattle as of the hanging up of the receiver, a short sharp click and a ring, and I realised that he had gone.

The next morning in response to a telegraphic summons my stenographer arrived and when I explained the situation to him he was incredulous, but orders were orders and he remained. I could see, however, that as nine o'clock approached he grew visibly nervous, which indicated that he half believed me anyhow, and when at nine to the second the sharp ring of the 'phone fell upon our ears he jumped as if he had been shot.

"Hello," said I again. "That you, Baron?"

"The same," the voice replied. "Stenographer ready?"

"Yes," said I.

The stenographer walked to the desk, placed the receiver at his ear, and with trembling voice announced his presence. There was a response of some kind, and then more calmly he remarked,

" Fire ahead, Mr. Munchausen," and began to write rapidly in short-hand.

Two days later he handed me a type-written copy of the following stories. The reader will observe that they are in the form of interviews, and it should be stated here that they appeared originally in the columns of the Sunday edition of the *Gehenna Gazette,* a publication of Hades which circulates wholly among the best people of that country, and which, if report saith truly, would not print a line which could not be placed in the hands of children, and to whose columns such writers as Chaucer, Shakespeare, Ben Jonson, Jonah and Ananias are frequent contributors.

Indeed, on the statement of Mr. Munchausen, all the interviews herein set forth were between himself as the principal and the Hon. Henry B. Ananias as reporter, or were scrupulously edited by the latter before being published.

THE SPORTING TOUR OF MR. MUNCHAUSEN

"GOOD morning, Mr. Munchausen," said the interviewer of the *Gehenna Gazette* entering the apartment of the famous traveller at the Hotel Deville, where the late Baron had just arrived from his sporting tour in the Blue Hills of Cimmeria and elsewhere.

"The interests of truth, my dear Ananias," replied the Baron, grasping me cordially by the hand, " require that I should state it as my opinion that it is not a good morning. In fact, my good friend, it is a very bad morning. Can you not see that it is raining cats and dogs without?"

" Sir," said I with a bow, " I accept the spirit of your correction but not the letter. It is raining indeed, sir, as you suggest, but having passed through it myself on my way hither I can personally testify that it is raining rain, and not a single cat or canine has, to my knowledge, as yet fallen from the clouds to the parched earth, although I am

13

informed that down upon the coast an elephant and three cows have fallen upon one of the summer hotels and irreparably damaged the roof."

Mr. Munchausen laughed.

"It is curious, Ananias," said he, "what sticklers for the truth you and I have become."

"It is indeed, Munchausen," I returned. "The effects of this climate are working wonders upon us. And it is just as well. You and I are out-classed by these twentieth century prevaricators concerning whom late arrivals from the upper world tell such strange things. They tell me that lying has become a business and is no longer ranked among the Arts or Professions."

"Ah me!" sighed the Baron with a retrospective look in his eye, "lying isn't what it used to be, Ananias, in your days and mine. I fear it has become one of the lost arts."

"I have noticed it myself, my friend, and only last night I observed the same thing to my well beloved Sapphira, who was lamenting the transparency of the modern lie, and said that lying to-day is no better than the truth. In our day a prevarication

14

had all of the opaque beauty of an opalescent bit of glass, whereas to-day in the majority of cases it is like a great vulgar plate-glass window, through which we can plainly see the ugly truths that lie behind. But, sir, I am here to secure from you not a treatise upon the lost art of lying, but some idea of the results of your sporting tour. You fished, and hunted, and golfed, and doubtless did other things. You, of course, had luck and made the greatest catch of the season; shot all the game in sight, and won every silver, gold and pewter golf mug in all creation?"

"You speak truly, Ananias," returned Mr. Munchausen. "My luck *was* wonderful—even for one who has been so singularly fortunate as I. I took three tons of speckled beauties with one cast of an ordinary horse whip in the Blue Hills, and with nothing but a silken line and a minnow hook landed upon the deck of my steam yacht a whale of most tremendous proportions; I shot game of every kind in great abundance and in my golf there was none to whom I could not give with ease seven holes in every nine and beat him out."

" Seven? " said I, failing to see how the ex-Baron could be right

" Seven," said he complacently. " Seven on the first, and seven on the second nine; fourteen in all of the eighteen holes."

" But," I cried, " I do not see how that could be. With fourteen holes out of the eighteen given to your opponent even if you won all the rest you still would be ten down."

" True, by ordinary methods of calculation," returned the Baron, " but I got them back on a technicality, which I claim is a new and valuable discovery in the game. You see it is impossible to play more than one hole at a time, and I invariably proved to the Greens Committee that in taking fourteen holes at once my opponent violated the physical possibilities of the situation. In every case the point was accepted as well taken, for if we allow golfers to rise above physical possibilities the game is gone. The integrity of the Card is the soul of Golf," he added sententiously.

" Tell me of the whale," said I, simply. " You landed a whale of large proportions on the deck of your yacht with a simple silken line and a minnow hook."

"Well it's a tough story," the Baron replied, handing me a cigar. "But it is true, Ananias, true to the last word. I was fishing for eels. Sitting on the deck of *The Lyre* one very warm afternoon in the early stages of my trip, I baited a minnow hook and dropped it overboard. It was the roughest day at sea I had ever encountered. The waves were mountain high, and it is the sad fact that one of our crew seated in the main-top was drowned with the spray of the dashing billows. Fortunately for myself, directly behind my deck chair, to which I was securely lashed, was a powerful electric fan which blew the spray away from me, else I too might have suffered the same horrid fate. Suddenly there came a tug on my line. I was half asleep at the time and let the line pay out involuntarily, but I was wide-awake enough to know that something larger than an eel had taken hold of the hook. I had hooked either a Leviathan or a derelict. Caution and patience, the chief attributes of a good angler were required   I hauled the line in until it

17

was taut. There were a thousand yards of it out, and when it reached the point of tensity, I gave orders to the engineers to steam closer to the object at the other end. We steamed in five hundred yards, I meanwhile hauling in my line. Then came another tug and I let out ten yards. 'Steam closer,' said I. 'Three hundred yards sou—sou-west by nor'-east.' The yacht obeyed on the instant. I called the Captain and let him feel the line. 'What do you think it is?' said I. He pulled a half dozen times. 'Feels like a snag,' he said, 'but seein' as there ain't no snags out here, I think it must be a fish.' 'What kind?' I asked. I could not but agree that he was better acquainted with the sea and its denizens than I. 'Well,' he replied, 'it is either a sea serpent or a whale.' At the mere mention of the word whale I was alert. I have always wanted to kill a whale. 'Captain,' said I, 'can't you tie an anchor onto a hawser, and bait the flukes with a boa constrictor and make sure of him?' He looked at me contemptuously. 'Whales eats fish,' said he, 'and they don't bite at no anchors. Whales has brains, whales has.' 'What shall we do?' I asked. 'Steam closer,' said the Captain, and we did so."

Munchausen took a long breath and for the moment was silent.

"Well?" said I.

"Well, Ananias," said he. "We resolved to wait. As the Captain said to me, 'Fishin' is waitin'.' So we waited. 'Coax him along,' said the Captain. 'How can we do it?' I asked. 'By kindness,' said he. 'Treat him gently, persuasive-like and he'll come.' We waited four days and nobody moved and I grew weary of coaxing. 'We've got to do something,' said I to the Captain. 'Yes,' said he, 'Let's *make* him move. He doesn't seem to respond to kindness.' 'But how?' I cried. 'Give him an electric shock,' said the Captain. 'Telegraph him his mother's sick and may be it'll move him.' 'Can't you get closer to him?' I demanded, resent-ing his facetious manner. 'I can, but it will scare him off,' replied the Captain. So we turned all our batteries on the sea. The dynamo shot forth its bolts and along about four o'clock in the afternoon there was the whale drawn by magnetic influence to the side of *The Lyre*. He was a beauty, Ananias," Munchausen added with enthusiasm. " You never saw such a whale. His back was as broad as the deck of an ocean steamer and in his length he exceeded the dimensions of *The Lyre* by sixty feet."

" And still you got him on deck? " I asked,—I, Ananias, who can stand something in the way of an exaggeration.

" Yes," said Munchausen, lighting his cigar, which had gone out. " Another storm came up and we rolled and rolled and rolled, until I thought *The Lyre* was going to capsize."

" But weren't you sea-sick? " I asked.

" Didn't have a chance to be," said Munchausen. " I was thinking of the whale all the time. Finally there came a roll in which we went completely under, and with a slight pulling on the line the whale was landed by the force of the wave and laid squarely upon the deck."

" Great Sapphira! " said I. " But you just said he was wider and longer than the yacht! "

" He was," sighed Munchausen. " He landed on

20

"There was the whale drawn by magnetic
influence to the side of *The Lyre*."

Chapter II.

the deck and by sheer force of his weight the yacht went down under him. I swam ashore and the whole crew with me. The next day Mr. Whale floated in strangled. He'd swallowed the thousand yards of line and it got so tangled in his tonsils that it choked him to death. Come around next week and I'll give you a couple of pounds of whale-bone for Mrs. Ananias, and all the oil you can carry."

I thanked the old gentleman for his kind offer and promised to avail myself of it, although as a newspaper man it is against my principles to accept gifts from public men.

"It was great luck, Baron," said I. "Or at least it would have been if you hadn't lost your yacht."

"That was great luck too," he observed noncha-lantly. "It cost me ten thousand dollars a month keeping that yacht in commission. Now she's gone I save all that. Why it's like finding money in the street, Ananias. She wasn't worth more than fifty thousand dollars, and in six months I'll be ten thousand ahead."

I could not but admire the cheerful philosophy

21

of the man, but then I was not surprised. Munchausen was never the sort of man to let little things worry him.

"But that whale business wasn't a circumstance to my catch of three tons of trout with a single cast of a horse-whip in the Blue Hills," said the Baron after a few moments of meditation, during which I could see that he was carefully marshalling his facts.

"I never heard of its equal," said I. "You must have used a derrick."

"No," he replied suavely. "Nothing of the sort. It was the simplest thing in the world. It was along about five o'clock in the afternoon when with my three guides and my valet I drove up the winding roadway of Great Sulphur Mountain on my way to the Blue Mountain House where I purposed to put up for a few days. I had one of those big mountain wagons with a covered top to it such as the pioneers used on the American plains, with six fine horses to the fore. I held the reins myself, since we were in the midst of a terrific thunderstorm and I felt safer when I did my own driving.

All the flaps of the leathern cover were let down at the sides and at the back, and were securely fastened. The roads were unusually heavy, and when we came to the last great hill before the lake all but I were walking, as a measure of relief to the horses. Suddenly one of the horses balked right in the middle of the ascent, and in a moment of impatience I gave him a stinging flick with my whip, when like a whirlwind the whole six swerved to one side and started on a dead run upward. The jolt and the unexpected swerving of the wagon threw me from my seat and I landed clear of the wheels in the soft mud of the roadway, fortunately without injury. When I arose the team was out of sight and we had to walk the remainder of the distance to the hotel. Imagine our surprise upon arriving there to find the six panting steeds and the wagon standing before the main entrance to the hotel dripping as though they had been through the Falls of Niagara, and, would you believe it, Ananias, inside that leather cover of the wagon, packed as tightly as sardines, were no less than three thousand trout, not one of them weighing less than a pound and some of them getting as high as four. The whole catch weighed a trifle over six thousand pounds."

"Great Heavens, Baron," I cried. "Where the dickens did they come from?"

"That's what I asked myself," said the Baron easily. "It seemed astounding at first glance, but investigation showed it after all to be a very simple proposition. The runaways after reaching the top of the hill turned to the left, and clattered on down toward the bridge over the inlet to the lake. The bridge broke beneath their weight and the horses soon found themselves struggling in the water. The harness was strong and the wagon never left them. They had to swim for it, and I am told by a small boy who was fishing on the lake at the time that they swam directly across it, pulling the wagon after them. Naturally with its open front and confined back and sides the wagon acted as a sort of drag-net and when the opposite shore was gained, and the wagon was pulled ashore, it was found to have gathered in all the fish that could not get out of the way."

The Baron resumed his cigar, and I sat still eyeing the ample pattern of the drawing-room carpet.

" Pretty good catch for an afternoon, eh?" he said in a minute.

"Yes," said I. "Almost too good, Baron. Those horses must have swam like the dickens to get over so quickly. You would think the trout would have had time to escape."

"Oh I presume one or two of them did," said Munchausen. " But the majority of them couldn't. The horses were all fast, record-breakers anyhow. I never hire a horse that isn't."

And with that I left the old gentleman and walked blushing back to the office. I don't doubt for an instant the truth of the Baron's story, but somehow or other I feel that in writing it my reputation is in some measure at stake.

NOTE—Mr. Munchausen, upon request of the Editor of the *Gehenna Gazette* to write a few stories of adventure for his Imp's page, conducted by Sapphira, contributed the tales which form the substance of several of the following chapters.

III

THREE MONTHS IN A BALLOON

MR. MUNCHAUSEN was not handsome, but the Imps liked him very much, he was so full of wonderful reminiscences, and was always willing to tell anybody that would listen, all about himself. To the Heavenly Twins he was the greatest hero that had ever lived. Napoleon Bonaparte, on Mr. Munchausen's own authority, was not half the warrior that he, the late Baron had been, nor was Cæsar in his palmiest days, one-quarter so wise or so brave. How old the Baron was no one ever knew, but he had certainly lived long enough to travel the world over, and stare every kind of death squarely in the face without flinching. He had fought Zulus, Indians, tigers, elephants—in fact, everything that fights, the Baron had encountered, and in every contest he had come out victorious. He was the only man the children had ever seen that had lost three legs in battle and then had recov-

26

ered them after the fight was over; he was the only visitor to their house that had been lost in the African jungle and wandered about for three months without food or shelter, and best of all he was, on his own confession, the most truthful narrator of extraordinary tales living. The youngsters had to ask the Baron a question only, any one, it mattered not what it was—to start him off on a story of adventure, and as he called upon the Twins' father once a month regularly, the children were not long in getting together a collection of tales beside which the most exciting episodes in history paled into insignificant commonplaces.

" Uncle Munch," said the Twins one day, as they climbed up into the visitor's lap and disarranged his necktie, " was you ever up in a balloon? "

" Only once," said the Baron calmly. " But I had enough of it that time to last me for a life-time."

" Was you in it for long? " queried the Twins, taking the Baron's watch out of his pocket and flinging it at Cerberus, who was barking outside of the window.

27

"Well, it seemed long enough," the Baron answered, putting his pocket-book in the inside pocket of his vest where the Twins could not reach it. "Three months off in the country sleeping all day long and playing tricks all night seems a very short time, but three months in a balloon and the constant centre of attack from every source is too long for comfort."

"Were you up in the air for three whole months?" asked the Twins, their eyes wide open with astonishment.

"All but two days," said the Baron. "For two of those days we rested in the top of a tree in India. The way of it was this: I was always, as you know, a great favourite with the Emperor Napoleon, of France, and when he found himself involved in a war with all Europe, he replied to one of his courtiers who warned him that his army was not in condition: 'Any army is prepared for war whose commander-in-chief numbers Baron Munchausen among his advisers. Let me have Munchausen at my right hand and I will fight the world.' So they sent for me and as I was not very busy I concluded to go and assist the French, although the allies and I were also very good friends. I reasoned it out this way: In this fight the allies are the stronger. They do not need me. Napoleon does. Fight for the weak, Munchausen, I said to myself, and so I went. Of course, when I reached Paris I went at once to the Emperor's palace and remained at his side until he took the field, after which I remained behind for a few days to put things to rights for the Imperial family. Unfortunately for the French, the King of Prussia heard of my delay in going to the front, and he sent word to his forces to intercept me on my way to join Napoleon at all hazards, and this they tried to do. When I was within ten miles of the Emperor's headquarters, I was stopped by the Prussians, and had it not been that I had provided myself with a balloon for just such an emergency, I should have been captured and confined in the King's palace at Berlin, until the war was over.

"Foreseeing all this, I had brought with me a large balloon packed away in a secret section of my trunk, and while my body-guard was fighting with the Prussian troops sent to capture me, I and my valet inflated the balloon, jumped into the car and were soon high up out of the enemy's reach. They fired several shots at us, and one of them would have pierced the balloon had I not, by a rare good shot, fired my own rifle at the bullet, and hitting it squarely in the middle, as is my custom, diverted it from its course, and so saved our lives.

"It had been my intention to sail directly over the heads of the attacking party and drop down into Napoleon's camp the next morning, but unfortunately for my calculations, a heavy wind came up in the night and the balloon was caught by a northerly blast, and blown into Africa, where, poised in the air directly over the desert of Sahara, we encountered a dead calm, which kept us stalled up for two miserable weeks."

"Why didn't you come down?" asked the Twins, "wasn't the elevator running?"

"We didn't dare," explained the Baron, ignoring the latter part of the question. "If we had we'd have wasted a great deal of our gas, and our condition would have been worse than ever. As I told you we were directly over the centre of the desert. There was no way of getting out of it except by long and wearisome marches over the hot, burning sands with the chances largely in favour of our never getting out alive. The only thing to do was to stay just where we were and wait for a favouring breeze. This we did, having to wait four mortal weeks before the air was stirred."

"You said two weeks a minute ago, Uncle Munch," said the Twins critically.

"Two? Hem! Well, yes it was two, now that I think of it. It's a natural mistake," said the Baron stroking his mustache a little nervously. "You see two weeks in a balloon over a vast desert of sand, with nothing to do but whistle for a breeze, is equal to four weeks anywhere else. That is, it seems so. Anyhow, two weeks or four, whichever it was, the breeze came finally, and along about midnight left us stranded again directly over an Arab encampment near Wady Halfa. It was a more perilous position really, than the first, because the moment the Arabs caught sight of us they began to make frantic efforts to get us down. At first we simply laughed them to scorn and made faces at them, because as far as we could see, we were safely out of reach. This enraged them and they apparently made up their minds to kill us if they could. At first their idea was to get us down alive and sell us as slaves, but our jeers changed all that, and what should they do but whip out a lot of guns and begin to pepper us.

" ' I'll settle them in a minute,' I said to myself, and set about loading my own gun. Would you believe it, I found that my last bullet was the one with which I had saved the balloon from the Prussian shot? "

" Mercy, how careless of you, Uncle Munch! " said one of the Twins. " What did you do? "

" I threw out a bag of sand ballast so that the balloon would rise just out of range of their guns, and then, as their bullets got to their highest point and began to drop back, I reached out and caught them in a dipper. Rather neat idea, eh? With these I loaded my own rifle and shot every one of the hostile party with their own ammunition, and when the last of the attacking Arabs dropped

I found there were enough bullets left to fill the empty sand bag again, so that the lost ballast was not missed. In fact, there were enough of them in weight to bring the balloon down so near to the earth that our anchor rope dangled directly over the encampment, so that my valet and I, without wasting any of our gas, could climb down and secure all the magnificent treasures in rugs and silks and rare jewels these robbers of the desert had managed to get together in the course of their depredations. When these were placed in the car another breeze came up, and for the rest of the time we drifted idly about in the heavens waiting for a convenient place to land. In this manner we were blown hither and yon for three months over land and sea, and finally we were wrecked upon a tall tree in India, whence we escaped by means of a convenient elephant that happened to come our way, upon which we rode triumphantly into Calcutta. The treasures we had secured from the Arabs, unfortunately, we had to leave behind us in the tree, where I suppose they still are. I hope some day to go back and find them."

Here Mr. Munchausen paused for a moment to catch his breath. Then he added with a sigh. " Of course, I went back to France immediately, but by the time I reached Paris the war was over, and the Emperor was in exile. I was too late to save him—though I think if he had lived some sixty or seventy years longer I should have managed to restore his throne, and Imperial splendour to him."

The Twins gazed into the fire in silence for a minute or two. Then one of them asked:

" But what did you live on all that time, Uncle Munch? "

" Eggs," said the Baron. " Eggs and occasionally fish. My servant had had the foresight when getting the balloon ready to include, among the things put into the car, a small coop in which were six pet chickens I owned, and without which I never went anywhere. These laid enough eggs every day to keep us alive. The fish we caught when our balloon stood over the sea, baiting our anchor with pieces of rubber gas pipe used to inflate the balloon, and which looked very much like worms."

34

"As their bullets got to their highest point and began to drop back, I reached out and caught them."

Chapter III.

" But the chickens? " said the Twins. " What did they live on? "

The Baron blushed.

" I am sorry you asked that question," he said, his voice trembling somewhat. " But I'll answer it if you promise never to tell anyone. It was the only time in my life that I ever practised an intentional deception upon any living thing, and I have always regretted it, although our very lives depended upon it."

" What was it, Uncle Munch? " asked the Twins, awed to think that the old warrior had ever deceived anyone.

" I took the egg shells and ground them into powder, and fed them to the chickens. The poor creatures supposed it was corn-meal they were getting," confessed the Baron. " I know it was mean, but what could I do? "

" Nothing," said the Twins softly. " And we don't think it was so bad of you after all. Many another person would have kept them laying eggs until they starved, and then he'd have killed them and eaten them up. You let them live."

35

"That may be so," said the Baron, with a smile that showed how relieved his conscience was by the Twins' suggestion. "But I couldn't do that you know, because they were pets. I had been brought up from childhood with those chickens."

Then the Twins, jamming the Baron's hat down over his eyes, climbed down from his lap and went to their play, strongly of the opinion that, though a bold warrior, the Baron was a singularly kind, soft-hearted man after all.

IV

SOME HUNTING STORIES FOR CHILDREN

THE Heavenly Twins had been off in the mountains during their summer holiday, and in consequence had seen very little of their good old friend, Mr. Munchausen. He had written them once or twice, and they had found his letters most interesting, especially that one in which he told how he had killed a moose up in Maine with his Waterbury watch spring, and I do not wonder that they marvelled at that, for it was one of the most extraordinary happenings in the annals of the chase. It seems, if his story is to be believed, and I am sure that none of us who know him has ever had any reason to think that he would deceive intentionally; it seems, I say, that he had gone to Maine for a week's sport with an old army acquaintance of his, who had now become a guide in that region. Unfortunately his rifle, of which he was very fond, and with which his aim was unerring, was in some manner mislaid on the way, and when they arrived in the woods they were utterly without weapons; but Mr.

Munchausen was not the man to be daunted by any such trifle as that, particularly while his friend had an old army musket, a relic of the war, stored away in the attic of his woodland domicile.

" Th' only trouble with that ar musket," said the old guide, " ain't so much that she won't shoot straight, nor that she's got a kick onto her like an unbroke mule. What I'm most afeard 'on about your shootin' with her ain't that I think she'll bust neither, for the fact is we ain't got nothin' for to bust her with, seein' as how ammynition is skeerce. I got powder, an' I got waddin', but I ain't got no shot."

" That doesn't make any difference," the Baron replied. " We can make the shot. Have you got any plumbing in the camp? If you have, rip it out, and I'll melt up a water-pipe into bullets."

" No, sir," retorted the old man. " Plumbin' is one of the things I came here to escape from."

" Then," said the Baron, " I'll use my watch for ammunition. It is only a three-dollar watch and I can spare it."

With this determination, Mr. Munchausen took

his watch to pieces, an ordinary time-piece of the old-fashioned kind, and, to make a long story short, shot for several days with the component parts of that useful affair rammed down into the barrel of the old musket. With the stem-winding ball he killed an eagle; with pieces of the back cover chopped up to a fineness of medium-sized shot he brought down several other birds, but the great feat of all was when he started for moose with nothing but the watch-spring in the barrel of the gun. Having rolled it up as tight as he could, fastened it with a piece of twine, and rammed it well into the gun, he set out to find the noble animal upon whose life he had designs. After stalking the woods for several hours, he came upon the tracks which told him that his prey was not far off, and in a short while he caught sight of a magnificent creature, his huge antlers held proudly up and his great eyes full of defiance.

For a moment the Baron hesitated. The idea of destroying so beautiful an animal seemed to be abhorrent to his nature, which, warrior-like as he is, has something of the tenderness of a woman about it. A second glance at the superb creature, however, changed all that, for the Baron then saw that to shoot to kill was necessary, for the beast was about to force a fight in which the hunter himself would be put upon the defensive.

" I won't shoot you through the head, my beauty," he said, softly, " nor will I puncture your beautiful coat with this load of mine, but I'll kill you in a new way."

With this he pulled the trigger. The powder exploded, the string binding the long black spring into a coil broke, and immediately the strip of steel shot forth into the air, made directly toward the neck of the rushing moose, and coiling its whole sinuous length tightly about the doomed creature's throat strangled him to death.

As the Twins' father said, a feat of that kind entitled the Baron to a high place in fiction at least, if not in history itself. The Twins were very much wrought up over the incident, particularly, when one too-smart small imp who was spending the summer at the same hotel where they were said that he didn't believe it,—but he was an imp who had never seen a cheap watch, so how should he know anything about what could be done with a spring that cannot be wound up by a great strong man in less than ten minutes?

As for the Baron he was very modest about the achievement, for when he first appeared at the Twins' home after their return he had actually forgotten all about it, and, in fact, could not recall the incident at all, until Diavolo brought him his own letter, when, of course, the whole matter came back to him.

" It wasn't so very wonderful, anyhow," said the Baron. " I should not think, for instance, of bragging about any such thing as that. It was a simple affair all through."

" And what did you do with the moose's antlers? " asked Angelica. " I hope you brought 'em home with you, because I'd like to see 'em."

" I wanted to," said the Baron, stroking the Twins' soft brown locks affectionately. " I wanted to bring them home for your father to use as a hat rack, dear, but they were too large. When I had removed them from the dead animal, I found

41

them so large that I could not get them out of the forest, they got so tangled up in the trees. I should have had to clear a path twenty feet wide and seven miles long to get them even as far as my friend's hut, and after that they would have had to be carried thirty miles through the woods to the express office."

"I guess it's just as well after all," said Diavolo. "If they were as big as all that, Papa would have had to build a new house to get 'em into."

"Exactly," said the Baron. "Exactly. That same idea occurred to me, and for that reason I concluded not to go to the trouble of cutting away those miles of trees. The antlers would have made a very expensive present for your father to receive in these hard times."

"It was a good thing you had that watch," the Twins observed, after thinking over the Baron's adventure. "If you hadn't had that you couldn't have killed the moose."

"Very likely not," said the Baron, "unless I had been able to do as I did in India thirty years ago at a man hunt."

42

"What?" cried the Twins. "Do they hunt men in India?"

"That all depends, my dears," replied the Baron. "It all depends upon what you mean by the word they. Men don't hunt men, but animals, great wild beasts sometimes hunt them, and it doesn't often happen that the men escape. In the particular man hunt I refer to I was the creature that was being hunted, and I've had a good deal of sympathy for foxes ever since. This was a regular fox hunt in a way, although I was the fox, and a herd of elephants were the huntsmen."

"How queer," said Diavolo, unscrewing one of the Baron's shirt studs to see if he would fall apart.

"Not half so queer as my feelings when I realised my position," said the Baron with a shake of his head. "I was frightened half to death. It seemed to me that I'd reached the end of my tether at last. I was studying the fauna and flora of India, in a small Indian village, known as ah—what was the name of that town! Ah—something like Rathabad —no, that isn't quite it—however, one name does as well as another in India. It was a good many

43

miles from Calcutta, and I'd been living there about three months. The village lay in a small valley between two ranges of hills, none of them very high. On the other side of the westerly hills was a great level stretch of country upon which herds of elephants used to graze. Out of this rose these hills, very precipitously, which was a very good thing for the people in the valley, else those elephants would have come over and played havoc with their homes and crops. To me the plains had a great fascination, and I used to wander over them day after day in search of new specimens for my collection of plants and flowers, never thinking of the danger I ran from an encounter with these elephants, who were very ferocious and extremely jealous of the territory they had come through years of occupation to regard as their own. So it happened, that one day, late in the afternoon, I was returning from an expedition over the plains, and, as I had found a large number of new specimens, I was feeling pretty happy. I whistled loudly as I walked, when suddenly coming to a slight undulation in the plain what should I see before me but a herd of sixty-three elephants, some eating, some thinking, some romping, and some lying asleep on the soft turf. Now, if I had come quietly, of course, I could have passed them unobserved, but as I told you I was whistling. I forget what the tune was, The Marsellaise or Die Wacht Am Rhein, or maybe Tommie Atkins, which enrages the elephants very much, being the national anthem of the British invader. At any rate, whatever the tune was it attracted the attention of the elephants, and then their sport began. The leader lifted his trunk high in the air, and let out a trumpet blast that echoed back from the cliff three miles distant. Instantly every elephant was on the alert. Those that had been sleeping awoke, and sprang to their feet. Those that had been at play stopped in their romp, and under the leadership of the biggest brute of the lot they made a rush for me. I had no gun; nothing except my wits and my legs with which to defend myself, so I naturally began to use the latter until I could get the former to work. It was nip

45

and tuck. They could run faster than I could, and I saw in an instant that without stratagem I could not hope to reach a place of safety. As I have said, the cliff, which rose straight up from the plain like a stone-wall, was three miles away, nor was there any other spot in which I could find a refuge. It occurred to me as I ran that if I ran in circles I could edge up nearer to the cliff all the time, and still keep my pursuers at a distance for the simple reason that an elephant being more or less unwieldy cannot turn as rapidly as a man can, so I kept running in circles. I could run around my short circle in less time than the enemy could run around his larger one, and in this manner I got nearer and nearer my haven of safety, the bellowing beasts snorting with rage as they followed. Finally, when I began to see that I was tolerably safe, another idea occurred to me, which was that if I could manage to kill those huge creatures the ivory I could get would make my fortune. But how! That was the question. Well, my dearly beloved Imps, I admit that I am a fast runner, but I am

" I got nearer and nearer my haven of safety,
the bellowing beasts snorting with rage as
they followed."

Chapter IV.

also a fast thinker, and in less than two minutes I had my plan arranged. I stopped short when about two hundred feet from the cliff, and waited until the herd was fifty feet away. Then I turned about and ran with all my might up to within two feet of the cliff, and then turning sharply to the left ran off in that direction. The elephants, thinking they had me, redoubled their speed, but failed to notice that I had turned, so quickly was that move· ment executed. They failed likewise to notice the cliff, as I had intended. The consequence was the whole sixty-three of them rushed head first, bang! with all their force, into the rock. The hill shook with the force of the blow and the sixty-three ele- phants fell dead. They had simply butted their brains out."

Here the Baron paused and pulled vigourously on his cigar, which had almost gone out.

" That was fine," said the Twins.

" What a narrow escape it was for you, Uncle Munch," said Diavolo.

" Very true," said the great soldier rising, as a

47

signal that his story was done. "In fact you might say that I had sixty-three narrow escapes, one for each elephant."

"But what became of the ivory?" asked Angelica.

"Oh, as for that!" said the Baron, with a sigh, "I was disappointed in that. They turned out to be all young elephants, and they had lost their first teeth. Their second teeth hadn't grown yet. I got only enough ivory to make one paper cutter, which is the one I gave your father for Christmas last year."

Which may account for the extraordinary interest the Twins have taken in their father's paper cutter ever since.

V

"DID you ever own a dog, Baron Munchausen?" asked the reporter of the *Gehenna Gazette,* calling to interview the eminent nobleman during Dog Show Week in Cimmeria.

" Yes, indeed I have," said the Baron, " I fancy I must have owned as many as a hundred dogs in my life. To be sure some of the dogs were iron and brass, but I was just as fond of them as if they had been made of plush or lamb's wool. They were so quiet, those iron dogs were; and the brass dogs never barked or snapped at any one."

" I never saw a brass dog," said the reporter. " What good are they?"

" Oh they are likely to be very useful in winter," the Baron replied. " My brass dogs used to guard my fire-place and keep the blazing logs from rolling out into my room and setting fire to the rug the Khan of Tartary gave me for saving his life from a herd of Antipodes he and I were hunting in the Himalaya Mountains."

" I don't see what you needed dogs to do that for," said the reporter. " A fender would have done just as well, or a pair of andirons," he added.

" That's what these dogs were," said the Baron. " They were fire dogs and fire dogs are andirons."

Ananias pressed his lips tightly together, and into his eyes came a troubled look. It was evident that, revolting as the idea was to him, he thought the Baron was trying to deceive him. Noting his displeasure, the Baron inwardly resolving to be careful how he handled the truth, hastened on with his story.

" But dogs were never my favourite animals," he said. " With my pets I am quite as I am with other things. I like to have pets that are entirely different from the pets of other people, and that is why in my day I have made companions of such animals as the sangaree, and the camomile, and the—ah— the two-horned piccolo. I've had tame bees even— in fact my bees used to be the wonder of Siam, in which country I was stationed for three years, having been commissioned by a British company to make a study of its climate with a view to finding

out if it would pay the company to go into the ice
business there. Siam is, as you have probably
heard, a very warm country, and as ice is a very
rare thing in warm countries these English people
thought they might make a vast fortune by sending
tug-boats up to the Arctic Ocean, and with them
capture and tow icebergs to Siam, where they
might be cut up and sold to the people at tremendous profit. The scheme was certainly a good one,
and I found many of the wealthy Siamese quite
willing to subscribe for a hundred pounds of ice a
week at ten dollars a pound, but it never came to
anything because we had no means of preserving
the icebergs after we got them into the Gulf of
Siam. The water was so hot that they melted before we could cut them up, and we nearly got ourselves into very serious trouble with the coast
people for that same reason. An iceberg, as you
know, is a huge affair, and when a dozen or two of
them had melted in the Gulf they added so to the
quantity of water there that fifty miles of the
coast line were completely flooded, and thousands
of valuable fish, able to live in warm water only,

were so chilled that they got pneumonia, and died. You can readily imagine how indignant the Siamese fishermen were with my company over the losses they had to bear, but their affection for me personally was so great that they promised not to sue the company if I would promise not to let the thing occur again. This I promised, and all went well. But about the bees, it was while I was living in Bangkok that I had them, and they were truly wonderful. There was hardly anything those bees couldn't do after I got them tamed."

"How did you tame them, Baron," asked Ananias.

"Power of the eye, my boy," returned the Baron. "I attracted their attention first and then held it. Of course, I tried my plan on one bee first. He tamed the rest. Bees are very like children. They like to play stunts—I think it is called stunts, isn't it, when one boy does something, and all his companions try to do the same thing?"

"Yes," said Ananias, "I believe there is such a game, but I shouldn't like to play it with you."

"Well, that was the way I did with the bees,"

said Mr. Munchausen. " I tamed the king bee, and when he had learned all sorts of funny little tricks, such as standing on his head and humming tunes, I let him go back to the swarm. He was gone a week, and then he came back, he had grown so fond of me—as well he might, because I fed him well, giving him a large basket of flowers three times a day. Back with him came two or three thousand other bees, and whatever Jang did they did."

" Who was Jang? " asked Ananias.

" That was the first bee's name. King Jang. Jang is Siamese for Billie, and as I was always fond of the name, Billie, I called him Jang. By and by every bee in the lot could hum the Star Spangled Banner and Yankee Doodle as well as you or I could, and it was grand on those soft moonlight nights we had there, to sit on the back porch of my pagoda and listen to my bee orchestra discoursing sweet music. Of course, as soon as Jang had learned to hum one tune it was easy enough for him to learn another, and before long the bee orchestra could give us any bit of music we wished

53

to have. Then I used to give musicales at my house and all the Siamese people, from the King down asked to be invited, so that through my pets my home became one of the most attractive in all Asia.

"And the honey those bees made! It was the sweetest honey you ever tasted, and every morning when I got down to breakfast there was a fresh bottleful ready for me, the bees having made it in the bottle itself over night. They were the most grateful pets I ever had, and once they saved my life. They used to live in a hive I had built for them in one corner of my room and I could go to bed and sleep with every door in my house open, and not be afraid of robbers, because those bees were there to protect me. One night a lion broke loose from the Royal Zoo, and while trotting along the road look-ing for something to eat he saw my front door wide open. In he walked, and began to sniff. He sniffed here and he sniffed there, but found nothing but a pot of anchovy paste, which made him thirstier and hungrier than ever. So he prowled into the parlour, and had his appetite further aggravated by a bronze statue of the Emperor of China I had there. He thought in the dim light it was a small-sized human being, and he pounced on it in a minute. Well, of course, he couldn't make any headway trying to eat a bronze statue, and the more he tried the more hungry and angry he got. He roared until he shook the house and would undoubtedly have awakened me had it not been that I am always a sound sleeper and never wake until I have slept enough. Why, on one occasion, on the Northern Pacific Railway, a train I was on ran into and completely telescoped another while I was asleep in the smoking car, and although I was severely burned and hurled out of the car window to land sixty feet away on the prairie, I didn't wake up for two hours. I was nearly buried alive because they thought I'd been killed, I lay so still.

" But to return to the bees. The roaring of the lion disturbed them, and Jang buzzed out of his hive to see what was the matter just as the lion appeared at my bed-room door. The intelligent insect saw in a moment what the trouble was, and he sounded the alarm for the rest of the bees, who came swarming out of the hive in response to the sum-

55

mons. Jang kept his eye on the lion meanwhile, and just as the prowler caught sight of your uncle peacefully snoring away on the bed, dreaming of his boyhood, and prepared to spring upon me, Jang buzzed over and sat down upon his back, putting his sting where it would do the most good. The angry lion, who in a moment would have fastened his teeth upon me, turned with a yelp of pain, and the bite which was to have been mine wrought havoc with his own back. Following Jang's example, the other bees ranged themselves in line over the lion's broad shoulders, and stung him until he roared with pain. Each time he was stung he would whisk his head around like a dog after a flea, and bite himself, until finally he had literally chewed himself up, when he fainted from sheer exhaustion, and I was saved. You can imagine my surprise when next morning I awakened to find a dying lion in my room."

"But, Baron," said Ananias. "I don't understand one thing about it. If you were fast asleep while all this was happening how did you know that Jang did those things?"

"Jang buzzed over and sat down upon his back, putting his sting where it would do the most good."

Chapter V.

"Why, Jang told me himself," replied the Baron calmly.

"Could he talk?" cried Ananias in amazement.

"Not as you and I do," said the Baron. "Of course not, but Jang could spell. I taught him how. You see I reasoned it out this way. If a bee can be taught to sing a song which is only a story in music, why can't he be taught to tell a story in real words. It was worth trying anyhow, and I tried. Jang was an apt pupil. He was the most intelligent bee I ever met, and it didn't take me more than a month to teach him his letters, and when he once knew his letters it was easy enough to teach him how to spell. I got a great big sheet and covered it with twenty-six squares, and in each of these squares I painted a letter of the alphabet, so that finally when Jang came to know them, and wanted to tell me anything he would fly from one square to another until he had spelled out whatever he wished to say. I would follow his movements closely, and we got so after awhile that we could converse for hours without any trouble whatsoever. I really believe that if Jang had been a little heavier so that he

57

could push the keys down far enough he could have
managed a typewriter as well as anybody, and
when I think about his wonderful mind and delicious fancy I deeply regret that there never was a
typewriting machine so delicately made that a bee
of his weight could make it go. The world would
have been very much enriched by the stories Jang
had in his mind to tell, but it is too late now. He
is gone forever."

"How did you lose Jang, Baron?" asked
Ananias, with tears in his eyes.

"He thought I had deceived him," said the
Baron, with a sigh. "He was as much of a stickler
for truth as I am. An American friend of mine
sent me a magnificent parterre of wax flowers
which were so perfectly made that I couldn't tell
them from the real. I was very proud of them,
and kept them in my room near the hive. When
Jang and his tribe first caught sight of them they
were delighted and they sang as they had never
sung before just to show how pleased they were.
Then they set to work to make honey out of them.

They must have laboured over those flowers for two months before I thought to tell them that they were only wax and not at all real. As I told Jang this, I unfortunately laughed, thinking that he could understand the joke of the thing as well as I, but I was mistaken. All that he could see was that he had been deceived, and it made him very angry. Bees don't seem to have a well-developed sense of humour. He cast a reproachful glance at me and returned to his hive and on the morning of the third day when I waked up they were moving out. They flew to my lattice and ranged themselves along the slats and waited for Jang. In a moment he appeared and at a given signal they buzzed out of my sight, humming a farewell dirge as they went. I never saw them again."

Here the Baron wiped his eyes.

"I felt very bad about it," he went on, "and resolved then never again to do anything which even suggested deception, and when several years later I had my crest designed I had a bee drawn on it, for in my eyes my good friend the bee, represents

three great factors of the good and successful life—
Industry, Fidelity, and Truth."

Whereupon the Baron went his way, leaving
Ananias to think it over.

HE TELLS THE TWINS OF FIRE-WORKS

THERE was a great noise going on in the public square of Cimmeria when Mr. Munchausen
sauntered into the library at the home of the Heavenly Twins.

" These Americans are having a great time of it
celebrating their Fourth of July," said he, as the
house shook with the explosion of a bomb.
" They've burnt powder enough already to set ten
revolutions revolving, and they're going to outdo
themselves to-night in the park. They've made a
bicycle out of the two huge pin-wheels, and they're
going to make Benedict Arnold ride a mile on it
after it's lit."

The Twins appeared much interested. They too
had heard much of the celebration and some of its
joys and when the Baron arrived they were primed
with questions.

" Uncle Munch," they said, helping the Baron to
remove his hat and coat, which they threw into
a corner so anxious were they to get to work, " do

61

you think there's much danger in little boys having fire-crackers and rockets and pin-wheels, or in little girls having torpeters?"

"Well, I don't know," the Baron answered, warily. "What does your venerable Dad say about it?"

"He thinks we ought to wait until we are older, but we don't," said the Twins.

"Torpeters never sets nothing afire," said Angelica.

"That's true," said the Baron, kindly; "but after all your father is right. Why do you know what happened to me when I was a boy?"

"You burnt your thumb," said the Twins, ready to make a guess at it.

"Well, you get me a cigar, and I'll tell you what happened to me when I was a boy just because my father let me have all the fire-works I wanted, and then perhaps you will see how wise your father is in not doing as you wish him to," said Mr. Munchausen.

The Twins readily found the desired cigar, after which Mr. Munchausen settled down comfortably in the hammock, and swinging softly to and fro, told his story.

" My dear old father," said he, " was the most indulgent man that ever lived. He'd give me anything in the world that I wanted whether he could afford it or not, only he had an original system of giving which kept him from being ruined by indulgence of his children. He gave me a Rhine steamboat once without its costing him a cent. I saw it, wanted it, was beginning to cry for it, when he patted me on the head and told me I could have it, adding, however, that I must never take it away from the river or try to run it myself. That satisfied me. All I wanted really was the happiness of feeling it was mine, and my dear old daddy gave me permission to feel that way. The same thing happened with reference to the moon. He gave it to me freely and ungrudgingly. He had received it from his father, he said, and he thought he had owned it long enough. Only, he added, as he had about the steamboat, I must leave it where it was and let other people look at it whenever they wanted to, and not interfere if I found any other little boys or girls playing with its beams, which I promised and have faithfully observed to this day.

"Of course from such a parent as this you may very easily see everything was to be expected on such a day as the Tenth of August which the people in our region celebrated because it was my birthday. He used to let me have my own way at all times, and it's a wonder I wasn't spoiled. I really can't understand how it is that I have become the man I am, considering how I was indulged when I was small.

"However, like all boys, I was very fond of celebrating the Tenth, and being a more or less ingenious lad, I usually prepared my own fire-works and many things happened which might not otherwise have come to pass if I had been properly looked after as you are. The first thing that happened to me on the Tenth of August that would have a great deal better not have happened, was when I was—er—how old are you Imps?"

"Sixteen," said they. "Going on eighteen."

"Nonsense," said the Baron. "Why you're not more than eight."

"Nope—we're sixteen," said Diavolo. "I'm eight and Angelica's eight and twice eight is sixteen."

"Oh," said the Baron. "I see. Well, that was exactly the age I was at the time. Just eight to a day."

"Sixteen we said," said the Twins.

"Yes," nodded the Baron. "Just eight, but going on towards sixteen. My father had given me ten thalers to spend on noises, but unlike most boys I did not care so much for noises as I did for novelties. It didn't give me any particular pleasure to hear a giant cracker go off with a bang. What I wanted to do most of all was to get up some kind of an exhibition that would please the people and that could be seen in the day-time instead of at night when everybody is tired and sleepy. So instead of spending my money on fire-crackers and torpedoes and rockets, I spent nine thalers of it on powder and one thaler on putty blowers. My particular object was to make one grand effort and provide passers-by with a free exhibition of what I was going to call 'Munchausen's Grand Geyser

Cascade.' To do this properly I had set my eye upon a fish pond not far from the town hall. It was a very deep pond and about a mile in circumference, I should say. Putty blowers were then selling at five for a pfennig and powder was cheap as sand owing to the fact that the powder makers, expecting a war, had made a hundred times as much as was needed, and as the war didn't come off, they were willing to take almost anything they could get for it. The consequence was that the powder I got was sufficient in quantity to fill a rubber bag as large as five sofa cushions. This I sank in the middle of the pond, without telling anybody what I intended to do, and through the putty blowers, sealed tightly together end to end, I conducted a fuse, which I made myself, from the powder bag to the shore. My idea was that I could touch the thing off, you know, and that about sixty square feet of the pond would fly up into the air and then fall gracefully back again like a huge fountain. If it had worked as I expected everything would have been all right, but it didn't. I had too much powder, for a second after I had lit the fuse there came a muffled roar and the whole pond in a solid mass, fish and all, went flying up into the air and disappeared. Everybody was astonished, not a few were very much frightened. I was scared to death but I never let on to any one that I was the person that had blown the pond off. How high the pond went I don't know, but I do know that for a week there wasn't any sign of it, and then most unexpectedly out of what appeared to be a clear sky there came the most extraordinary rain-storm you ever saw. It literally poured down for two days, and, what I alone could understand, with it came trout and sunfish and minnows, and most singular to all but myself an old scow that was recognised as the property of the owner of the pond suddenly appeared in the sky falling toward the earth at a fearful rate of speed. When I saw the scow coming I was more frightened than ever because I was afraid it might fall upon and kill some of our neighbours. Fortunately, however, this possible disaster was averted, for it came down directly over the sharp-pointed lightning-rod on the tower of our public library and stuck there like a piece of paper on a file.

"The rain washed away several acres of finely cultivated farms, but the losses on crops and fences and so forth were largely reduced by the fish that came with the storm. One farmer took a rake and caught three hundred pounds of trout, forty pounds of sun-fish, eight turtles, and a minnow in his potato patch in five minutes. Others were almost as fortunate, but the damage was sufficiently large to teach me that parents cannot be too careful about what they let their children do on the day they celebrate."

"And weren't you ever punished?" asked the Twins.

"No, indeed," said the Baron. "Nobody ever knew that I did it because I never told them. In fact you are the only two persons who ever heard about it, and you mustn't tell, because there are still a number of farmers around that region who would sue me for damages in case they knew that I was responsible for the accident."

"Out of what appeared to be a clear sky
came the most extraordinary rain storm you
ever saw."

Chapter VI.

"That was pretty awful," said the Twins. "But we don't want to blow up ponds so as to get cascadeses, but we do want torpeters. Torpeters aren't any harm, are they, Uncle Munch?"

"Well, you can never tell. It all depends on the torpedo. Torpedoes are sometimes made carelessly," said the Baron. "They ought to be made as carefully as a druggist makes pills. So many pebbles, so much paper, and so much saltpeter and sulphur, or whatever else is used to make them go off. I had a very unhappy time once with a carelessly made torpedo. I had two boxes full. They were those tin-foil torpedoes that little girls are so fond of, and I expected they would make quite a lot of noise, but the first ten I threw down didn't go off at all. The eleventh for some reason or other, I never knew exactly what, I hurled with all my force against the side of my father's barn, and my, what a surprise it was! It smashed in the whole side of the barn and sent seven bales of hay, and our big farm plough bounding down the hillside into the town. The hay-bales smashed down fences; one of them hit a cow-shed on its way down, knocked the back of it to smithereens and then proceeded to demolish the rear end of a small crockery shop that fronted on the main street. It struck the crockery shop square in the middle of its back and threw down fifteen dozen cups and saucers, thirty-two water pitchers, and five china busts of Shakespeare. The din was frightful—but I couldn't help that. Nobody could blame me, because I had no means of knowing that the man who made the torpedoes was careless and had put a solid ball of dynamite into one of them. So you see, my dear Imps, that even torpedoes are not always safe."

"Yes," said Angelica. "I guess I'll play with my dolls on my birthday. They never goes off and blows things up."

"That's very wise of you," said the Baron.

"But what became of the plough, Uncle Munch?" said Diavolo.

"Oh, the plough didn't do much damage," replied Mr. Munchausen. "It simply furrowed its way down the hill, across the main street, to the bowling green. It ploughed up about one hundred feet of this before it stopped, but nobody minded that much because it was to have been ploughed and seeded again anyhow within a few days. Of course the furrow it made in crossing the road was bad, and to make it worse the share caught one of the water pipes that ran under the street, and ripped it in two so that the water burst out and flooded the street for a while, but one hundred and sixty thousand dollars would have covered the damage."

The Twins were silent for a few moments and then they asked:

" Well, Uncle Munch, what kind of fire-works are safe anyhow? "

" My experience has taught me that there are only two kinds that are safe," replied their old friend. " One is a Jack-o-lantern and the other is a cigar, and as you are not old enough to have cigars, if you will put on your hats and coats and go down into the garden and get me two pumpkins, I'll make each of you a Jack-o'-lantern. What do you say? "

" We say yes," said the Twins, and off they went,

71

while the Baron turning over in the hammock, and arranging a pillow comfortably under his head, went to sleep to dream of more birthday recollections in case there should be a demand for them later on.

VII

SAVED BY A MAGIC LANTERN

WHEN the Sunday dinner was over, the Twins, on Mr. Munchausen's invitation, climbed into the old warrior's lap, Angelica kissing him on the ear, and Diavolo giving his nose an affectionate tweak.

"Ah!" said the Baron. "That's it!"

"What's what, Uncle Munch?" demanded Diavolo.

"Why that," returned the Baron. "I was wondering what it was I needed to make my dinner an unqualified success. There was something lacking, but what it was, we have had so much, I could not guess until you two Imps kissed me and tweaked my nasal feature. Now I know, for really a feeling of the most blessed contentment has settled upon my soul."

"Don't you wish *you* had two youngsters like us, Uncle Munch?" asked the Twins.

"Do I wish I had? Why I have got two young-

73

sters like you," the Baron replied. "I've got 'em right here too."

"Where?" asked the Twins, looking curiously about them for the other two.

"On my knees, of course," said he. "You are mine. Your papa gave you to me—and you are as like yourselves as two peas in a pod."

"I—I hope you aren't going to take us away from here," said the Twins, a little ruefully. They were very fond of the Baron, but they didn't exactly like the idea of being given away.

"Oh no—not at all," said the Baron. "Your father has consented to keep you here for me and your mother has kindly volunteered to look after you. There is to be no change, except that you belong to me, and, vice versa, I belong to you."

"And I suppose, then," said Diavolo, "if you belong to us you've got to do pretty much what we tell you to?"

"Exactly," responded Mr. Munchausen. "If you should ask me to tell you a story I'd have to do it, even if you were to demand the full particulars of how I spent Christmas with Mtulu, King of the Taafe Eatars, on the upper Congo away down in Africa—which is a tale I have never told any one in all my life."

" It sounds as if it might be interesting," said the Twins. " Those are real candy names, aren't they? "

" Yes," said the Baron. " Taafe sounds like taffy and Mtulu is very suggestive of chewing gum. That's the curious thing about the savage tribes of Africa. Their names often sound as if they might be things to eat instead of people. Perhaps that is why they sometimes eat each other—though, of course, I won't say for sure that that is the real explanation of cannibalism."

" What's cannon-ballism? " asked Angelica.

" He didn't say cannon-ballism," said Diavolo, scornfully. " It was candy-ballism."

" Well—you've both come pretty near it," said the Baron, " and we'll let the matter rest there, or I won't have time to tell you how Christmas got me into trouble with King Mtulu."

The Baron called for a cigar, which the Twins lighted for him and then he began.

"You may not have heard," he said, "that some twenty or thirty years ago I was in command of an expedition in Africa. Our object was to find Lake Majolica, which we hoped would turn up half way between Lollokolela and the Clebungo Mountains. Lollokolela was the furthermost point to which civilisation had reached at that time, and was directly in the pathway to the Clebungo Mountains, which the natives said were full of gold and silver mines and scattered all over which were reputed to be caves in which diamonds and rubies and other gems of the rarest sort were to be found in great profusion. No white man had ever succeeded in reaching this marvellously rich range of hills for the reason that after leaving Lollokolela there was, as far as was known, no means of obtaining water, and countless adventurous spirits had had to give up because of the overpowering thirst which the climate brought upon them.

"Under such circumstances it was considered by a company of gentlemen in London to be well worth their while to set about the discovery of a lake, which they decided in advance to call Majolica, for

76

reasons best known to themselves; they probably wanted to jar somebody with it. And to me was intrusted the mission of leading the expedition. I will confess that I did not want to go for the very good reason that I did not wish to be eaten alive by the savage tribes that infested that region, but the company provided me with a close fitting suit of mail, which I wore from the time I started until I returned. It was very fortunate for me that I was so provided, for on three distinct occasions I was served up for state dinners and each time successfully resisted the carving knife and as a result, was thereafter well received, all the chiefs looking upon me as one who bore a charmed existence."

Here the Baron paused long enough for the Twins to reflect upon and realise the terrors which had beset him on his way to Lake Majolica, and be it said that if they had thought him brave before they now deemed him a very hero of heroes.

"When I set out," said the Baron, "I was accompanied by ten Zanzibaris and a thousand tins of condensed dinners."

"A thousand what, Uncle Munch?" asked Jack, his mouth watering.

"Condensed dinners," said the Baron, "I had a lot of my favourite dinners condensed and put up in tins. I didn't expect to be gone more than a year and a thousand dinners condensed and tinned, together with the food I expected to find on the way, elephant meat, rhinoceros steaks, and tiger chops, I thought would suffice for the trip. I could eat the condensed dinners and my followers could have the elephant's meat, rhinoceros steaks, and tiger chops—not to mention the bananas and other fruits which grow wild in the African jungle. It was not long, however, before I made the discovery that the Zanzibaris, in order to eat tigers, need to learn first how to keep tigers from eating them. We went to bed late one night on the fourth day out from Lollokolela, and when we waked up the next morning every mother's son of us, save myself, had been eaten by tigers, and again it was nothing but my coat of mail that saved me. There were eighteen tigers' teeth sticking into the sleeve of the coat, as it was. You can imagine my distress

78

at having to continue the search for Lake Majolica alone. It was then that I acquired the habit of talking to myself, which has kept me young ever since, for I enjoy my own conversation hugely, and find myself always a sympathetic listener. I walked on for days and days, until finally, on Christmas Eve, I reached King Mtulu's palace. Of course your idea of a palace is a magnificent five-story building with beautiful carvings all over the front of it, marble stair-cases and handsomely painted and gilded ceilings. King Mtulu's palace was nothing of the sort, although for that region it was quite magnificent, the walls being decorated with elephants' tusks, crocodile teeth and many other treasures such as delight the soul of the Central African.

" Now as I may not have told you, King Mtulu was the fiercest of the African chiefs, and it is said that up to the time when I outwitted him no white man had ever encountered him and lived to tell the tale. Consequently, when without knowing it on this sultry Christmas Eve, laden with the luggage and the tinned dinners and other things I had brought with me I stumbled upon the blood-thirsty monarch I gave myself up for lost.

" 'Who comes here to disturb the royal peace?' cried Mtulu, savagely, as I crossed the threshold.

" 'It is I, your highness,' I returned, my face blanching, for I recognized him at once by the ivory ring he wore in the end of his nose.

" 'Who is I?' retorted Mtulu, picking up his battle axe and striding forward.

" A happy thought struck me then. These folks are superstitious. Perhaps the missionaries may have told these uncivilised creatures the story of Santa Claus. I will pretend that I am Santa Claus. So I answered, 'Who is I, O Mtulu, Bravest of the Taafe Chiefs? I am Santa Claus, the Children's Friend, and bearer of gifts to and for all.'

" Mtulu gazed at me narrowly for a moment and then he beat lightly upon a tom-tom at his side. Immediately thirty of the most villainous-looking natives, each armed with a club, appeared.

" 'Arrest that man,' said Mtulu, 'before he goes any farther. He is an impostor.'

" 'If your majesty pleases,' I began.

" ' Silence! ' he cried, ' I am fierce and I eat men, but I love truth. The truthful man has nothing to fear from me, for I have been converted from my evil ways and since last New Year's day I have eaten only those who have attempted to deceive me. You will be served raw at dinner to-morrow night. My respect for your record as a man of courage leads me to spare you the torture of the frying-pan. You are Baron Munchausen. I recognized you the moment you turned pale. Another man would have blushed.'

" So I was carried off and shut up in a mud hovel, the interior walls of which were of white, a fact which strangely enough, preserved my life when later I came to the crucial moment. I had brought with me, among other things, for my amusement solely, a magic lantern. As a child, I had always been particularly fond of pictures, and when I thought of the lonely nights in Africa, with no books at hand, no theatres, no cotillions to enliven the monotony of my life, I resolved to take with me my little magic-lantern as much for company as for anything else. It was very compact in

81

form. It folded up to be hardly larger than a wallet containing a thousand one dollar bills, and the glass lenses of course could be carried easily in my trousers pockets. The views, instead of being mounted on glass, were put on a substance not unlike glass, but thinner, called gelatine. All of these things I carried in my vest pockets, and when Mtulu confiscated my luggage the magic lantern and views of course escaped his notice.

" Christmas morning came and passed and I was about to give myself up for lost, for Mtulu was not a king to be kept from eating a man by anything so small as a suit of mail, when I received word that before dinner my captor and his suite were going to pay me a formal parting call. Night was coming on and as I sat despondently awaiting the king's arrival, I suddenly bethought me of a lantern slide of the British army, standing and awaiting the command to fire, I happened to have with me. It was a superb view—lifelike as you please. Why not throw that on the wall and when Mtulu enters he will find me apparently with a strong force at my command, thought I. It was no sooner

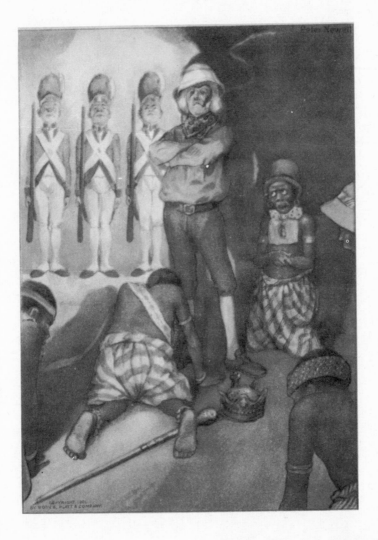

" ' I am your slave,' he replied to my greeting, kneeling before me, ' I yield all to you.' "

Chapter VII.

thought than it was done and my life was saved. Hardly was that noble picture reflected upon the rear wall of my prison when the door opened and Mtulu, followed by his suite, appeared. I rose to greet him, but apparently he saw me not. Mùte with terror he stood upon the threshold gazing at that terrible line of soldiers ready as he thought to sweep him and his men from the face of the earth with their death-dealing bullets.

"'I am your slave,' he replied to my greeting, kneeling before me, 'I yield all to you.'

"'I thought you would,' said I. 'But I ask nothing save the discovery of Lake Majolica. If within twenty-four hours Lake Majolica is not discovered I give the command to fire!' Then I turned and gave the order to carry arms, and lo! by a quick change of slides, the army appeared at a carry. Mtulu gasped with terror, but accepted my ultimatum. I was freed, Lake Majolica was discovered before ten o'clock the next morning, and at five o'clock I was on my way home, the British army reposing quietly in my breast pocket. It was a mighty narrow escape!"

"I should say so," said the Twins. "But Mtulu must have been awful stupid not to see what it was."

"Didn't he see through it when he saw you put the army in your pocket?" asked Diavolo.

"No," said the Baron, "that frightened him worse than ever, for you see he reasoned this way. If I could carry an army in my pocket-book, what was to prevent my carrying Mtulu himself and all his tribe off in the same way! He thought I was a marvellous man to be able to do that."

"Well, we guess he was right," said the Twins, as they climbed down from the Baron's lap to find an atlas and search the map of Africa for Lake Majolica. This they failed to find and the Baron's explanation is unknown to me, for when the Imps returned, the warrior had departed.

VIII

"THE editor has a sort of notion, Mr. Munchausen," said Ananias, as he settled down in the big arm-chair before the fire in the Baron's library, "that he'd like to have a story about a giraffe. Public taste has a necky quality about it of late."

"What do you say to that, Sapphira?" asked the Baron, politely turning to Mrs. Ananias, who had called with her husband. "Are you interested in giraffes?"

"I like lions better," said Sapphira. "They roar louder and bite more fiercely."

"Well, suppose we compromise," said the Baron, "and have a story about a poodle dog. Poodle dogs sometimes look like lions, and as a rule they are as gentle as giraffes."

"I know a better scheme than that," put in Ananias. "Tell us a story about a lion and a giraffe, and if you feel disposed throw in a few poodles for good measure. I'm writing on space this year."

"That's so," said Sapphira, wearily. "I could say it was a story about a lion and Ananias could call it a giraffe story, and we'd each be right."

"Very well," said the Baron, "it shall be a story of each, only I must have a cigar before I begin. Cigars help me to think, and the adventure I had in the Desert of Sahara with a lion, a giraffe, and a slippery elm tree was so long ago that I shall have to do a great deal of thinking in order to recall it."

So the Baron went for a cigar, while Ananias and Sapphira winked enviously at each other and lamented their lost glory. In a minute the Baron returned with the weed, and after lighting it, began his story.

"I was about twenty years old when this thing happened to me," said he. "I had gone to Africa to investigate the sand in the Desert of Sahara for a Sand Company in America. As you may already have heard, sand is a very useful thing in a great many ways, more particularly however in the building trades. The Sand Company was

formed for the purpose of supplying sand to everybody that wanted it, but land in America at that
time was so very expensive that there was very little profit in the business. People who owned sand
banks and sand lots asked outrageous prices for
their property; and the sea-shore people were not
willing to part with any of theirs because they
needed it in their hotel business. The great at-
traction of a seaside hotel is the sand on the beach,
and of course the proprietors weren't going to sell
that. They might better even sell their brass
bands. So the Sand Company thought it might be
well to build some steam-ships, load them with oysters, or mowing machines, or historical novels, or
anything else that is produced in the United States,
and in demand elsewhere; send them to Egypt, sell
the oysters, or mowing machines, or historical novels, and then have the ships fill up with sand from
the Sahara, which they could get for nothing, and
bring it back in ballast to the United States."

" It must have cost a lot! " said Ananias.

" Not at all," returned the Baron. " The profits
on the oysters and mowing machines and his-

torical novels were so large that all expenses both ways were more than paid, so that when it was delivered in America the sand had really cost less than nothing. We could have thrown it all overboard and still have a profit left. It was I who suggested the idea to the President of the Sand Company—his name was Bartlett, or—ah—Mulligan—or some similar well-known American name, I can't exactly recall it now. However, Mr. Bartlett, or Mr. Mulligan, or whoever it was, was very much pleased with the idea and asked me if I wouldn't go to the Sahara, investigate the quality of the sand, and report; and as I was temporarily out of employment I accepted the commission. Six weeks later I arrived in Cairo and set out immediately on a tour of the desert. I went alone because I preferred not to take any one into my confidence, and besides one can always be more independent when he has only his own wishes to consult. I also went on foot, for the reason that camels need a great deal of care—at least mine would have, if I'd had one, because I always like to have my steeds well groomed whether there is any one to see them or not. So to save myself trouble I started off alone on foot. In twenty-four hours I travelled over a hundred miles of the desert, and the night of the second day found me resting in the shade of a slippery elm tree in the middle of an oasis, which after much suffering and anxiety I had discovered. It was a beautiful moonlight night and I was enjoying it hugely. There were no mosqui- toes or insects of any kind to interfere with my comfort. No insects could have flown so far across the sands. I have no doubt that many of them have tried to get there, but up to the time of my arrival none had succeeded, and I felt as happy as though I were in Paradise.

" After eating my supper and taking a draught of the delicious spring water that purled up in the middle of the oasis, I threw myself down under the elm tree, and began to play my violin, without which in those days I never went anywhere."

" I didn't know you played the violin," said Sap- phira. " I thought your instrument was the trom- bone—plenty of blow and a mighty stretch."

" I don't—now," said the Baron, ignoring the

89

sarcasm. "I gave it up ten years ago—but that's a different story. How long I played that night I don't know, but I do know that lulled by the delicious strains of the music and soothed by the soft sweetness of the atmosphere I soon dropped off to sleep. Suddenly I was awakened by what I thought to be the distant roar of thunder. 'Humph!' I said to myself. 'This is something new. A thunder storm in the Desert of Sahara is a thing I never expected to see, particularly on a beautifully clear moonlight night'—for the moon was still shining like a great silver ball in the heavens, and not a cloud was anywhere to be seen. Then it occurred to me that perhaps I had been dreaming, so I turned over to go to sleep again. Hardly had I closed my eyes when a second ear-splitting roar came bounding over the sands, and I knew that it was no dream, but an actual sound that I heard. I sprang to my feet and looked about the horizon and there, a mere speck in the distance, was something—for the moment I thought a cloud, but in another instant I changed my mind, for glancing through my telescope I perceived it

was not a cloud but a huge lion with the glitter of
hunger in his eye. What I had mistaken for the
thunder was the roar of this savage beast. I seized
my gun and felt for my cartridge box only to discover that I had lost my ammunition and was there
alone, unarmed, in the great desert, at the mercy
of that savage creature, who was drawing nearer
and nearer every minute and giving forth the most
fearful roars you ever heard. It was a terrible
moment and I was in despair.

" ' It's all up with you, Baron,' I said to myself,
and then I caught sight of the tree. It seemed my
only chance. I must climb that. I tried, but alas!
As I have told you it was a slippery elm tree, and
I might as well have tried to climb a greased pole.
Despite my frantic efforts to get a grip upon the
trunk I could not climb more than two feet without slipping back. It was impossible. Nothing
was left for me to do but to take to my legs, and
I took to them as well as I knew how. My, what
a run it was, and how hopeless. The beast was
gaining on me every second, and before me lay mile
after mile of desert. ' Better give up and treat the

beast to a breakfast, Baron,' I moaned to myself.
'When there's only one thing to do, you might as
well do it and be done with it. Your misery will be
over the more quickly if you stop right here.' As I
spoke these words, I slowed up a little, but the
frightful roaring of the lion unnerved me for an
instant, or rather nerved me on to a spurt, which
left the lion slightly more to the rear—and which
resulted in the saving of my life; for as I ran on,
what should I see about a mile ahead but another
slippery elm tree, and under it stood a giraffe who
had apparently fallen asleep while browsing among
its upper branches, and filling its stomach with its
cooling cocoanuts. The giraffe had its back to me,
and as I sped on I formed my plan. I would grab
hold of the giraffe's tail; haul myself up onto his
back; climb up his neck into the tree, and then give
my benefactor a blow between the eyes which would
send him flying across the desert before the lion
could come along and get up into the tree the same
way I did. The agony of fear I went through as I
approached the long-necked creature was some-

thing dreadful. Suppose the giraffe should be awakened by the roaring of the lion before I got there and should rush off himself to escape the fate that awaited me? I nearly dropped, I was so nervous, and the lion was now not more than a hundred yards away. I could hear his breath as he came panting on. I redoubled my speed; his pants came closer, closer, until at length after what seemed a year, I reached the giraffe, caught his tail, raised myself up to his back, crawled along his neck and dropped fainting into the tree just as the lion sprang upon the giraffe's back and came on toward me. What happened then I don't know, for as I have told you I swooned away; but I do know that when I came to, the giraffe had disappeared and the lion lay at the foot of the tree dead from a broken neck."

" A broken neck? " demanded Sapphira.

" Yes," returned the Baron. " A broken neck! From which I concluded that as the lion reached the nape of the giraffe's neck, the giraffe had waked up and bent his head toward the earth, thus causing the lion to fall head first to the ground instead of landing as he had expected in the tree with me."

"It was wonderful," said Sapphira, scornfully.

"Yes," said Ananias, "but I shouldn't think a lion could break his neck falling off a giraffe. Perhaps it was one of the slippery elm cocoanuts that fell on him."

"Well, of course," said the Baron, rising, "that would all depend upon the height of the giraffe. Mine was the tallest one I ever saw."

"About how tall?" asked Ananias.

"Well," returned the Baron, thoughtfully, as if calculating, "did you ever see the Eiffel Tower?"

"Yes," said Ananias.

"Well," observed the Baron, "I don't think my giraffe was more than half as tall as that."

With which estimate the Baron bowed his guests out of the room, and with a placid smile on his face, shook hands with himself.

"Mr. and Mrs. Ananias are charming people," he chuckled, "but amateurs both—deadly amateurs."

" I reached the giraffe, raised myself to his
back, crawled along his neck and dropped
fainting into the tree."

Chapter VIII.

IX

DECORATION DAY IN THE CANNIBAL ISLANDS

"UNCLE MUNCH," said Diavolo as he clambered up into the old warrior's lap, "I don't suppose you could tell us a story about Decoration Day could you?"

"I think I might try," said Mr. Munchausen, puffing thoughtfully upon his cigar and making a ring with the smoke for Angelica to catch upon her little thumb. "I might try—but it will all depend upon whether you want me to tell you about Decoration Day as it is celebrated in the United States, or the way a band of missionaries I once knew in the Cannibal Islands observed it for twenty years or more."

"Why can't we have both stories?" said Angelica. "I think that would be the nicest way. Two stories is twice as good as one."

"Well, I don't know," returned Mr. Munchausen. "You see the trouble is that in the first instance I could tell you only what a beautiful thing it is that every year the people have a day set apart upon which they especially honour the memory of the noble fellows who lost their lives in defence of their country. I'm not much of a poet and it takes a poet to be able to express how beautiful and grand it all is, and so I should be afraid to try it. Besides it might sadden your little hearts to have me dwell upon the almost countless number of heroes who let themselves be killed so that their fellow-citizens might live in peace and happiness. I'd have to tell you about hundreds and hundreds of graves scattered over the battle fields that no one knows about, and which, because no one knows of them, are not decorated at all, unless Nature herself is kind enough to let a little dandelion or a daisy patch into the secret, so that they may grow on the green grass above these forgotten, unknown heroes who left their homes, were shot down and never heard of afterwards."

" Does all heroes get killed? " asked Angelica.

" No," said Mr. Munchausen. " I and a great many others lived through the wars and are living yet."

" Well, how about the missionaries? " said Diavolo. " I didn't know they had Decoration Day in the Cannibal Islands."

" I didn't either until I got there," returned the Baron. " But they have and they have it in July instead of May. It was one of the most curious things I ever saw and the natives, the men who used to be cannibals, like it so much that if the missionaries were to forget it they'd either remind them of it or have a celebration of their own. I don't know whether I ever told you about my first experience with the cannibals—did I? "

" I don't remember it, but if you had I would have," said Diavolo.

" So would I," said Angelica. " I remember most everything you say, except when I want you to say it over again, and even then I haven't forgotten it."

" Well, it happened this way," said the Baron. " It was when I was nineteen years old. I sort of thought at that time I'd like to be a sailor, and as my father believed in letting me try whatever I wanted to do I took a position as first mate of a steam brig that plied between San Francisco and

Nepaul, taking San Francisco canned tomatoes to Nepaul and bringing Nepaul pepper back to San Francisco, making several dollars both ways. Perhaps I ought to explain to you that Nepaul pepper is red, and hot; not as hot as a furnace fire, but hot enough for your papa and myself when we order oysters at a club and have them served so cold that we think they need a little more warmth to make them palatable and digestible. You are not yet old enough to know the meaning of such words as palatable and digestible, but some day you will be and then you'll know what your Uncle means. At any rate it was on the return voyage from Nepaul that the water tank on the *Betsy S.* went stale and we had to stop at the first place we could to fill it up with fresh water. So we sailed along until we came in sight of an Island and the Captain appointed me and two sailors a committee of three to go ashore and see if there was a spring anywhere about. We went, and the first thing we knew we were in the midst of a lot of howling, hungry savages, who were crazy to eat us. My companions were eaten, but when it came to my turn I tried to reason with the chief. 'Now see here, my friend,' said I, 'I'm perfectly willing to be served up at your breakfast, if I can only be convinced that you will enjoy eating me. What I don't want is to have my life wasted!' 'That's reasonable enough,' said he. 'Have you got a sample of yourself along for me to taste?' 'I have,' I replied, taking out a bottle of Nepaul pepper, that by rare good luck I happened to have in my pocket. 'That is a portion of my left foot powdered. It will give you some idea of what I taste like,' I added. 'If you like that, you'll like me. If you don't, you won't.' "

" That was fine," said Diavolo. " You told pretty near the truth, too, Uncle Munch, because you are hot stuff yourself, ain't you? "

" I am so considered, my boy," said Mr. Munchausen. " The chief took a teaspoonful of the pepper down at a gulp, and let me go when he recovered. He said he guessed I wasn't quite his style, and he thought I'd better depart before I set fire to the town. So I filled up the water bag, got into the row-boat, and started back to the ship, but the

Betsy S. had gone and I was forced to row all the way to San Francisco, one thousand, five hundred and sixty-two miles distant. The captain and crew had given us all up for lost. I covered the distance in six weeks, living on water and Nepaul pepper, and when I finally reached home, I told my father that, after all, I was not so sure that I liked a sailor's life. But I never forgot those cannibals or their island, as you may well imagine. They and their home always interested me hugely and I resolved if the fates ever drove me that way again, I would go ashore and see how the people were getting on. The fates, however, were a long time in drawing me that way again, for it was not until July, ten years ago that I reached there the second time. I was off on a yachting trip, with an English friend, when one afternoon we dropped anchor off that Cannibal Island.

" 'Let's go ashore,' said I. 'What for?' said my host; and then I told him the story and we went, and it was well we did so, for it was then and there that I discovered the new way the missionaries had of celebrating Decoration Day.

DECORATION DAY *with* CANNIBALS

" No sooner had we landed than we noticed that the Island had become civilised. There were churches, and instead of tents and mud-hovels, beautiful residences appeared here and there, through the trees. ' I fancy this isn't the island,' said my host. ' There aren't any cannibals about here.' I was about to reply indignantly, for I was afraid he was doubting the truth of my story, when from the top of a hill, not far distant, we heard strains of music. We went to see whence it came, and what do you suppose we saw? Five hundred villainous looking cannibals marching ten abreast along a fine street, and, cheering them from the balconies of the houses that fronted on the highway, were the missionaries and their friends and their children and their wives.

" ' This can't be the place, after all,' said my host again.

" ' Yes it is,' said I, ' only it has been converted. They must be celebrating some native festival.' Then as I spoke the procession stopped and the head missionary followed by a band of beautiful girls, came down from a platform and placed garlands of flowers and beautiful wreaths on the shoulders and heads of those reformed cannibals. In less than an hour every one of the huge black fellows was covered with roses and pinks and fragrant flowers of all kinds, and then they started on parade again. It was a fine sight, but I couldn't understand what it was all done for until that night, when I dined with the head missionary—and what do you suppose it was? "

" I give it up," said Diavolo, " maybe the missionaries thought the cannibals didn't have enough clothes on."

" I guess I can't guess," said Angelica.

" They were celebrating Decoration Day," said Mr. Munchausen. " They were strewing flowers on the graves of departed missionaries."

" You didn't tell us about any graves," said Diavolo.

" Why certainly I did," said the Baron. " The cannibals themselves were the only graves those poor departed missionaries ever had. Every one of those five hundred savages was the grave of a missionary, my dears, and having been converted, and

"They were celebrating Decoration Day
. . . . strewing flowers on the graves of departed missionaries."

Chapter IX.

taught that it was not good to eat their fellow-men, they did all in their power afterwards to show their repentance, keeping alive the memory of the men they had treated so badly by decorating themselves on memorial day—and one old fellow, the savagest looking, but now the kindest-hearted being in the world, used always to wear about his neck a huge sign, upon which he had painted in great black letters :

HERE LIES

JOHN THOMAS WILKINS,

SAILOR.

DEPARTED THIS LIFE, MAY 24TH, 1861.

HE WAS A MAN OF SPLENDID TASTE.

" The old cannibal had eaten Wilkins and later when he had been converted and realised that he himself was the grave of a worthy man, as an expiation he devoted his life to the memory of John

Thomas Wilkins, and as a matter of fact, on the Cannibal Island Decoration Day he would lie flat on the floor all the day, groaning under the weight of a hundred potted plants, which he placed upon himself in memory of Wilkins."

Here Mr. Munchausen paused for breath, and the twins went out into the garden to try to imagine with the aid of a few practical experiments how a cannibal would look with a hundred potted plants adorning his person.

MR. MUNCHAUSEN'S ADVENTURE WITH A SHARK

𝕸𝖗. 𝖆𝖓𝖉 𝕸𝖗𝖘. 𝖍𝖊𝖓𝖗𝖞 𝕭. 𝕬𝖓𝖆𝖓𝖎𝖆𝖘.

THURSDAYS.   **CIMMERIA.**

THIS was the card sent by the reporter of the *Gehenna Gazette,* and Mrs. Ananias to Mr. Munchausen upon his return from a trip to mortal realms concerning which many curious reports have crept into circulation. Owing to a rumour persistently circulated at one time, Mr. Munchausen had been eaten by a shark, and it was with the intention of learning, if possible, the basis for the rumour that Ananias and Sapphira called upon the redoubtable Baron of other days.

Mr. Munchausen graciously received the callers and asked what he could do for them.

" Our readers, Mr. Munchausen," explained An-

105

anias, " have been much concerned over rumours of your death at the hands of a shark."

" Sharks have no hands," said the Baron quietly.

" Well—that aside," observed Ananias. " Were you killed by a shark? "

" Not that I recall," said the Baron. " I may have been, but I don't remember it. Indeed I recall only one adventure with a shark. That grew out of my mission on behalf of France to the Czar of Russia. I carried letters once from the King of France to his Imperial Coolness the Czar."

" What was the nature of the letters? " asked Ananias.

" I never knew," replied the Baron. " As I have said, it was a secret mission, and the French Government never took me into its confidence. The only thing I know about it is that I was sent to St. Petersburg, and I went, and in the course of time I made myself much beloved of both the people and his Majesty the Czar. I am the only person that ever lived that was liked equally by both, and if I had attached myself permanently to the Czar, Russia would have been a different country to-day."

"What country would it have been, Mr. Munchausen," asked Sapphira innocently, "Germany or Siam?"

"I can't specify, my dear madame," the Baron replied. "It wouldn't be fair. But, at any rate, I went to Russia, and was treated warmly by everybody, except the climate, which was, as it is at all times, very freezing. That's the reason the Russian people like the climate. It is the only thing the Czar can't change by Imperial decree, and the people admire its independence and endure it for that reason. But as I have said, everybody was pleased with me, and the Czar showed me unusual attention. He gave fêtes in my honour. He gave the most princely dinners, and I met the very best people in St. Petersburg, and at one of these dinners I was invited to join a yachting party on a cruise around the world.

"Well, of course, though a landsman in every sense of the word, I am fond of yachting, and I immediately accepted the invitation. The yacht we went on was the Boomski Zboomah, belonging to Prince—er—now what was that Prince's name!

Something like—er—Sheeroff or Jibski—or—er—
well, never mind that. I meet so many princes it is
difficult to remember their names. We'll say his
name was Jibski."

"Suppose we do," said Ananias, with a jealous
grin. "Jibski is such a remarkable name. It will
look well in print."

"All right," said the Baron, "Jibski be it. The
yacht belonged to Prince Jibski, and she was a
beauty. There was a stateroom and a steward for
everybody on board, and nothing that could contrib-
ute to a man's comfort was left unattended to. We
set sail on the 23rd of August, and after cruising
about the North coast of Europe for a week or two,
we steered the craft south, and along about the
middle of September we reached the Amphibian
Islands, and anchored. It was here that I had my
first and last experience with sharks. If they had
been plain, ordinary sharks I'd have had an easy
time of it, but when you get hold of these Amphibian sharks you are likely to get yourself into
twenty-three different kinds of trouble."

ADVENTURE *with a* SHARK

"My!" said Sapphira. "All those? Does the number include being struck by lightning?"

"Yes," the Baron answered, "And when you remember that there are only twenty-four different kinds altogether you can see what a peck of trouble an Amphibian shark can get you into. I thought my last hour had come when I met with him. You see when we reached the Amphibian Islands, we naturally thought we'd like to go ashore and pick the cocoanuts and raisins and other things that grow there, and when I got upon dry land again I felt strongly tempted to go down upon the beautiful little beach in the harbour and take a swim. Prince Jibski advised me against it, but I was set upon going. He told me the place was full of sharks, but I wasn't afraid because I was always a remarkably rapid swimmer, and I felt confident of my ability, in case I saw a shark coming after me, to swim ashore before he could possibly catch me, provided I had ten yards start. So in I went leaving my gun and clothing on the beach. Oh, it was fun! The water was quite warm, and the

109

sandy bottom of the bay was deliciously soft and pleasant to the feet. I suppose I must have sported in the waves for ten or fifteen minutes before the trouble came. I had just turned a somersault in the water, when, as my head came to the surface, I saw directly in front of me, the unmistakable fin of a shark, and to my unspeakable dismay not more than five feet away. As I told you, if it had been ten yards away I should have had no fear, but five feet meant another story altogether. My heart fairly jumped into my mouth. It would have sunk into my boots if I had had them on, but I hadn't, so it leaped upward into my mouth as I turned to swim ashore, by which time the shark had reduced the distance between us by one foot. I feared that all was up with me, and was trying to think of an appropriate set of last words, when Prince Jibski, noting my peril, fired one of the yacht's cannon in our direction. Ordinarily this would have been useless, for the yacht's cannon was never loaded with anything but a blank charge, but in this instance it was better than if it had been loaded with ball and shot, for not only did the

110

sound of the explosion attract the attention of the shark and cause him to pause for a moment, but also the wadding from the gun dropped directly upon my back, so showing that Prince Jibski's aim was not as good as it might have been. Had the cannon been loaded with a ball or a shell, you can very well understand how it would have happened that yours truly would have been killed then and there."

"We should have missed you," said Ananias sweetly.

"Thanks," said the Baron. "But to resume. The shark's pause gave me the start I needed, and the heat from the burning wadding right between my shoulders caused me to redouble my efforts to get away from the shark and it, so that I never swam faster in my life, and was soon standing upon the shore, jeering at my fearful pursuer, who, strange to say, showed no inclination to stop the chase now that I was, as I thought, safely out of his reach. I didn't jeer very long I can tell you, for in another minute I saw why the shark didn't stop chasing me, and why Amphibian sharks are worse than any other kind. That shark had not only fins like all other sharks to swim with, but he had likewise three pairs of legs that he could use on land quite as well as he could use the fins in the water. And then began the prettiest chase you ever saw in your life. As he emerged from the water I grabbed up my gun and ran. Round and round the island we tore, I ahead, he thirty or forty yards behind, until I got to a place where I could stop running and take a hasty shot at him. Then I aimed, and fired. My aim was good, but struck one of the huge creature's teeth, broke it off short, and bounded off to one side. This made him more angry than ever, and he redoubled his efforts to catch me. I redoubled mine, until I could get another shot at him. The second shot, like the first, struck the creature in the teeth, only this time it was more effective. The bullet hit his jaw lengthwise, and knocked every tooth on that side of his head down his throat. So it went. I ran. He pursued. I fired; he lost his teeth, until finally I had knocked out every tooth he had, and then, of course, I wasn't afraid of him, and let him come up with me. With his teeth he could have ground me to atoms at one bite. Without them he was as powerless as a bowl of currant jelly, and when he opened his huge jaws, as he supposed to bite me in two, he was the most surprised looking fish you ever saw on land or sea to discover that the effect his jaws had upon my safety was about as great as had they been nothing but two feather bed mattresses."

" You must have been badly frightened, though," said Ananias.

" No," said the Baron. " I laughed in the poor disappointed thing's face, and with a howl of despair, he rushed back into the sea again. I made the best time I could back to the yacht for fear he might return with assistance."

" And didn't you ever see him again, Baron? " asked Sapphira.

" Yes, but only from the deck of the yacht as we were weighing anchor," said Mr. Munchausen. " I saw him and a dozen others like him doing precisely what I thought they would do, going ashore to search me out so as to have a little cold Munch for dinner. I'm glad they were disappointed, aren't you?"

"Yes, indeed," said Ananias and Sapphira, but not warmly.

Ananias was silent for a moment, and then walking over to one of the bookcases, he returned in a moment, bringing with him a huge atlas.

"Where are the Amphibian Islands, Mr. Munchausen?" he said, opening the book. "Show them to me on the map. I'd like to print the map with my story."

"Oh, I can't do that," said the Baron, "because they aren't on the map any more. When I got back to Europe and told the map-makers about the dangers to man on those islands, they said that the interests of humanity demanded that they be lost. So they took them out of all the geographies, and all the cyclopædias, and all the other books, so that nobody ever again should be tempted to go there; and there isn't a school-teacher or a sailor in the world to-day who could tell you where they are."

"But, you know, don't you?" persisted Ananias.

"Well, I did," said the Baron; "but, really I

114

"I laughed in the poor disappointed thing's face, and with a howl of despair he rushed back into the sea."

Chapter X.

have had to remember so many other things that I have forgotten that. All that I know is that they were named from the fact that they were infested by Amphibious animals, which are animals that can live on land as well as on water."

" How strange!" said Sapphira.

" It's just too queer for anything," said Ananias, " but on the whole I'm not surprised."

And the Baron said he was glad to hear it.

XI

THE BARON AS A RUNNER

THE Twins had been on the lookout for the Baron for at least an hour, and still he did not come, and the little Imps were beginning to feel blue over the prospect of getting the usual Sunday afternoon story. It was past four o'clock, and for as long a time as they could remember the Baron had never failed to arrive by three o'clock. All sorts of dreadful possibilities came up before their mind's eye. They pictured the Baron in accidents of many sorts. They conjured up visions of him lying wounded beneath the ruins of an apartment house, or something else equally heavy that might have fallen upon him on his way from his rooms to the station, but that he was more than wounded they did not believe, for they knew that the Baron was not the sort of man to be killed by anything killing under the sun.

"I wonder where he can be?" said Angelica, uneasily to her brother, who was waiting with equal anxiety for their common friend.

" Oh, he's all right! " said Diavolo, with a confidence he did not really feel. " He'll turn up all right, and even if he's two hours late he'll be here on time according to his own watch. Just you wait and see."

And they did wait and they did see. They waited for ten minutes, when the Baron drove up, smiling as ever, but apparently a little out of breath. I should not dare to say that he was really out of breath, but he certainly did seem to be so, for he panted visibly, and for two or three minutes after his arrival was quite unable to ask the Imps the usual question as to their very good health. Finally, however, the customary courtesies of the greeting were exchanged, and the decks were cleared for action.

" What kept you, Uncle Munch? " asked the Twins, as they took up their usual position on the Baron's knees.

" What what? " replied the warrior. " Kept me? Why, am I late? "

" Two hours," said the Twins. " Dad gave you up and went out for a walk."

117

" Nonsense," said the Baron. " I'm never that late."

Here he looked at his watch.

" Why I do seem to be behind time. There must be something wrong with our time-pieces. I can't be two hours late, you know."

" Well, let's say you are on time, then," said the Twins. " What kept you? "

" A very funny accident on the railroad," said the Baron lighting a cigar. " Queerest accident that ever happened to me on the railroad, too. Our engine ran away."

The Twins laughed as if they thought the Baron was trying to fool them.

" Really," said the Baron. " I left town as usual on the two o'clock train, which, as you know, comes through in half an hour, without a stop. Everything went along smoothly until we reached the Vitriol Reservoir, when much to the surprise of everybody the train came to a stand-still. I supposed there was a cow on the track, and so kept in my seat for three or four minutes as did every one else. Finally the conductor came through and

118

called to the brakeman at the end of our car to see if his brakes were all right.

" ' It's the most unaccountable thing,' he said to me. ' Here's this train come to a dead stop and I can't see why. There isn't a brake out of order on any one of the cars, and there isn't any earthly reason why we shouldn't go ahead.'

" ' Maybe somebody's upset a bottle of glue on the track,' said I. I always like to chaff the conductor, you know, though as far as that is concerned, I remember once when I was travelling on a South American Railway our train was stopped by highwaymen, who smeared the tracks with a peculiar sort of gum. They'd spread it over three miles of track, and after the train had gone lightly over two miles of it the wheels stuck so fast ten engines couldn't have moved it. That was a terrible affair."

" I don't think we ever heard of that, did we? " asked Angelica.

" I don't remember it," said Diavolo.

" Well, you would have remembered it, if you had ever heard of it," said the Baron. " It was too dreadful to be forgotten—not for us, you know,

119

but for the robbers. It was one of the Imperial trains in Brazil, and if it hadn't been for me the Emperor would have been carried off and held for ransom. The train was brought to a stand-still by this gluey stuff, as I have told you, and the desperadoes boarded the cars and proceeded to rifle us of our possessions. The Emperor was in the car back of mine, and the robbers made directly for him, but fathoming their intention I followed close upon their heels.

" ' You are our game,' said the chief robber, tapping the Emperor on the shoulder, as he entered the Imperial car.

" ' Hands off,' I cried throwing the ruffian to one side.

" He scowled dreadfully at me, the Emperor looked surprised, and another one of the robbers requested to know who was I that I should speak with so much authority. 'Who am I?' said I, with a wink at the Emperor. 'Who am I? Who else but Baron Munchausen of the Bodenwerder National Guard, ex-friend of Napoleon of France, intimate of the Mikado of Japan, and famed the

world over as the deadliest shot in two hemi-
spheres.'

"The desperadoes paled visibly as I spoke, and
after making due apologies for interfering with the
train, fled shrieking from the car. They had heard
of me before.

"'I thank you, sir,' began the Emperor, as the
would-be assassins fled, but I cut him short. 'They
must not be allowed to escape,' I said, and with that
I started in pursuit of the desperate fellows, over-
took them, and glued them with the gum they had
prepared for our detention to the face of a precipice
that rose abruptly from the side of the railway,
one hundred and ten feet above the level. There I
left them. We melted the glue from the tracks
by means of our steam heating apparatus, and were
soon booming merrily on our way to Rio Janeiro
when I was fêted and dined continuously for weeks
by the people, though strange to say the Emperor's
behaviour toward me was very cool."

"And did the robbers ever get down?" asked the
Twins.

"Yes, but not in a way they liked," Mr. Munchausen replied. "The sun came out, and after a week or two melted the glue that held them to the precipice, whereupon they fell to its base and were shattered into pieces so small there wasn't an atom of them to be found when a month later I passed that way again on my return trip."

"And didn't the Emperor treat you well, Uncle Munch?" asked the Imps.

"No—as I told you he was very cool towards me, and I couldn't understand it, then, but I do now," said the Baron. "You see he was very much in need of ready cash, the Emperor was, and as the taxpayers were already growling about the expenses of the Government he didn't dare raise the money by means of a tax. So he arranged with the desperadoes to stop the train, capture him, and hold him for ransom. Then when the ransom came along he was going to divide up with them. My sudden appearance, coupled with my determination to rescue him, spoiled his plan, you see, and so he naturally wasn't very grateful. Poor fellow, I was very sorry for it afterward, because he really was an excellent ruler, and his plan of raising the money he needed wasn't a bit less honest than most other ways rulers employ to obtain revenue for State purposes."

"Well, now, let's get back to the runaway engine," said the Twins. "You can tell us more about South America after you get through with that. How did the engine come to run away?"

"It was simple enough," said the Baron. "The engineer, after starting the train came back into the smoking car to get a light for his pipe, and while he was there the coupling-pin between the engine and the train broke, and off skipped the engine twice as fast as it had been going before. The relief from the weight of the train set its pace to a mile a minute instead of a mile in two minutes, and there we were at a dead stop in front of the Vitriol Station with nothing to move us along. When the engineer saw what had happened he fainted dead away, because you know if a collision had occurred between the runaway engine and the train ahead he would have been held responsible."

"Couldn't the fireman stop the engine?" asked the Twins.

123

"No. That is, it wouldn't be his place to do it, and these railway fellows are queer about that sort of thing," said the Baron. "The engineers would go out upon a strike if the railroad were to permit a stoker to manage the engine, and besides that the stoker wouldn't undertake to do it at a stoker's wages, so there wasn't any help to be looked for there. The conductor happened to be nearsighted, and so he didn't find out that the engine was missing until he had wasted ten or twenty minutes examining the brakes, by which time, of course, the runaway was miles and miles up the track. Then the engineer came to, and began to wring his hands and moan in a way that was heart-rending. The conductor, too, began to cry, and all the brakemen left the train and took to the woods. They weren't going to have any of the responsibility for the accident placed on their shoulders. Whether they will ever turn up again I don't know. But I realised as soon as anybody else that something had to be done, so I rushed into the telegraph office and telegraphed to all the station masters between the Vitriol Reservoir and Cimmeria to clear the track of all trains, freight, local, or express, or somebody would be hurt, and that I myself would undertake to capture the runaway engine. This they all promised to do, whereupon I bade good-bye to my fellow-travellers, and set off up the track myself at full speed. In a minute I strode past Sulphur Springs, covering at least eight ties at a stretch. In two minutes I thundered past Lava Hurst, where I learned that the engine had twenty miles start of me. I made a rapid calculation mentally—I always was strong in mental arithmetic, which showed that unless I was tripped up or got side-tracked somewhere I might overtake the runaway before it reached Noxmere. Redoubling my efforts, my stride increased to twenty ties at a jump, and I made the next five miles in two minutes. It sounds impossible, but really it isn't so. It is hard to run as fast as that at the start, but when you have got your start the impetus gathered in the first mile's run sends you along faster in the second, and so your speed increases by its own force until finally you go like the wind. At Gasdale I had gained two miles on the engine, at Sneakskill

I was only fifteen miles behind, and upon my arrival at Noxmere there was scarcely a mile between me and the fugitive. Unfortunately a large crowd had gathered at Noxmere to see me pass through, and some small boy had brought a dog along with him and the dog stood directly in my path. If I ran over the dog it would kill him and might trip me up. If I jumped with the impetus I had there was no telling where I would land. It was a hard point to decide either way, but I decided in favour of the jump, simply to save the dog's life, for I love animals. I landed three miles up the road and ahead of the engine, though I didn't know that until I had run ten miles farther on, leaving the engine a hundred yards behind me at every stride. It was at Miasmatica that I discovered my error and then I tried to stop. It was almost in vain; I dragged my feet over the ties, but could only slow down to a three-minute gait. Then I tried to turn around and slow up running backward; this brought my speed down ten minutes to the mile, which made it safe for me to run into a hay-stack at the side of the railroad just this side of Cimmeria.

126

"This brought my speed down ten minutes
to the mile, which made it safe for me to run
into a haystack."

Chapter XI.

Then, of course, I was all right. I could sit down and wait for the engine, which came booming along forty minutes later. As it approached I prepared to board it, and in five minutes was in full control. That made it easy enough for me to get back here without further trouble. I simply reversed the lever, and back we came faster than I can describe, and just one hour and a half from the time of the mishap the runaway engine was restored to its deserted train and I reached your station here in good order. I should have walked up, but for my weariness after that exciting run, which as you see left me very much out of breath, and which made it necessary for me to hire that worn-out old hack instead of walking up as is my wont."

"Yes, we see you are out of breath," said the Twins, as the Baron paused. "Would you like to lie down and take a rest?"

"Above all things," said the Baron. "I'll take a nap here until your father returns," which he proceeded at once to do.

While he slept the two Imps gazed at him curiously, Angelica, a little suspiciously.

127

" Bub," said she, in a whisper, " do you think that was a true story? "

" Well, I don't know," said Diavolo. " If anybody else than Uncle Munch had told it, I wouldn't have believed it. But he hates untruth. I know because he told me so."

" That's the way I feel about it," said Angelica. " Of course, he can run as fast as that, because he is very strong, but what I can't see is how an engine ever could run away from its train."

" That's what stumps me," said Diavolo.

MR. MUNCHAUSEN MEETS HIS MATCH

(Reported by Henry W. Ananias for the *Gehenna Gazette*.)

WHEN Mr. Munchausen, accompanied by Ananias and Sapphira, after a long and tedious journey from Cimmeria to the cool and wooded heights of the Blue Sulphur Mountains, entered the portals of the hotel where the greater part of his summers are spent, the first person to greet him was Beelzebub Sandboy,—the curly-headed Imp who acted as " Head Front " of the Blue Sulphur Mountain House, his eyes a-twinkle and his swift running feet as ever ready for a trip to any part of the hostelry and back. Beelzy, as the Imp was familiarly known, as the party entered, was in the act of carrying a half-dozen pitchers of iced-water upstairs to supply thirsty guests with the one thing needful and best to quench that thirst, and in his excitement at catching sight once again of his ancient friend the Baron, managed to drop two of the pitchers with a loud crash upon the office floor. This, however, was not noticed by the powers that ruled. Beelzy was not perfect, and as long as he smashed less than six pitchers a day on an average the management was disposed not to complain.

"There goes my friend Beelzy," said the Baron, as the pitchers fell. "I am delighted to see him. I was afraid he would not be here this year since I understand he has taken up the study of theology."

"Theology?" cried Ananias. "In Hades?"

"How foolish," said Sapphira. "We don't need preachers here."

"He'd make an excellent one," said Mr. Munchausen. "He is a lad of wide experience and his fish and bear stories are wonderful. If he can make them gee, as he would put it, with his doctrines he would prove a tremendous success. Thousands would flock to hear him for his bear stories alone. As for the foolishness of his choice, I think it is a very wise one. Everybody can't be a stoker, you know."

At any rate, whatever the reasons for Beelzebub's presence, whether he had given up the study of theology or not, there he was plying his old vocation with the same perfection of carelessness as of yore, and apparently no farther along in the study of theology than he was the year before when he bade Mr. Munchausen "good-bye forever" with the statement that now that he was going to lead a pious life the chances were he'd never meet his friend again.

"I don't see why they keep such a careless boy as that," said Sapphira, as Beelzy at the first landing turned to grin at Mr. Munchausen, emptying the contents of one of his pitchers into the lap of a nervous old gentleman in the office below.

"He adds an element of excitement to a not over-exciting place," explained Mr. Munchausen. "On stormy days here the men make bets on what fool thing Beelzy will do next. He blacked all the russet shoes with stove polish one year, and last season in the rush of his daily labours he filled up the water-cooler with soft coal instead of ice. He's a great bell-boy, is my friend Beelzy."

A little while later when Mr. Munchausen and his party had been shown to their suite, Beelzy appeared in their drawing-room and was warmly greeted by Mr. Munchausen, who introduced him to Mr. and Mrs. Ananias.

"Well," said Mr. Munchausen, "you're here again, are you?"

"No, indeed," said Beelzy. "I ain't here this year. I'm over at the Coal-Yards shovellin' snow. I'm my twin brother that died three years before I was born."

"How interesting," said Sapphira, looking at the boy through her lorgnette.

Beelzy bowed in response to the compliment and observed to the Baron:

"You ain't here yourself this season, be ye?"

"No," said Mr. Munchausen, drily. "I've gone abroad. You've given up theology I presume?"

"Sorter," said Beelzy. "It was lonesome business and I hadn't been at it more'n twenty minutes when I realised that bein' a missionary ain't all jam and buckwheats. It's kind o' dangerous too, and as I didn't exactly relish the idea o' bein' et up by Samoans an' Feejees I made up my mind to give it up an' stick to bell-boyin' for another season any how; but I'll see you later, Mr. Munchausen. I've got to hurry along with this iced-water. It's over-due now, and we've got the kickinest lot o' folks here this year you ever see. One man here the other night got as mad as hookey because it took forty minutes to soft bile an egg. Said two minutes was all that was necessary to bile an egg softer'n mush, not understanding anything about the science of eggs in a country where hens feeds on pebbles."

" Pebbles? " cried Mr. Munchausen. " What, do they lay Roc's eggs? "

Beelzy grinned.

" No, sir—they lay hen's eggs all right, but they're as hard as Adam's aunt."

" I never heard of chickens eating pebbles," observed Sapphira with a frown. " Do they really relish them? "

" I don't know, Ma'am," said Beelzy. " I ain't never been on speakin' terms with the hens, Ma'am, and they never volunteered no information. They eat 'em just the same. They've got to eat something and up here on these mountains there ain't anything but gravel for 'em to eat. That's why they do it. Then when it comes to the eggs, on **a** diet like that, cobblestones ain't in it with 'em for hardness, and when you come to bile 'em it takes a week to get 'em soft, an' a steam drill to get 'em open—an' this feller kicked at forty minutes! Most likely he's swearin' around upstairs now because this iced-water ain't came; and it ain't more than two hours since he ordered it neither."

"What an unreasonable gentleman," said Sapphira.

"Ain't he though!" said Beelzy. "And he ain't over liberal neither. He's been here two weeks now and all the money I've got out of him was a five-dollar bill I found on his bureau yesterday morning. There's more money in theology than there is in him."

With this Beelzebub grabbed up the pitcher of water, and bounded out of the room like a frightened fawn. He disappeared into the dark of the corridor, and a few moments later was evidently tumbling head over heels up stairs, if the sounds that greeted the ears of the party in the drawing-room meant anything.

The next morning when there was more leisure

for Beelzy the Baron inquired as to the state of his health.

"Oh it's been pretty good," said he. "Pretty good. I'm all right now, barrin' a little gout in my right foot, and ice-water on my knee, an' a crick in my back, an' a tired feelin' all over me generally. Ain't had much to complain about. Had the measles in December, and the mumps in February; an' along about the middle o' May the whoopin' cough got a holt of me; but as it saved my life I oughtn't to kick about that."

Here Beelzy looked gratefully at an invisible something—doubtless the recollection in the thin air of his departed case of whooping cough, for having rescued him from an untimely grave.

"That is rather curious, isn't it?" queried Sapphira, gazing intently into the boy's eyes. "I don't exactly understand how the whooping cough could save anybody's life, do you, Mr. Munchausen?"

"Beelzy, this lady would have you explain the situation, and I must confess that I am myself somewhat curious to learn the details of this wonderful rescue," said Mr. Munchausen.

" Well, I must say," said Beelzy, with a pleased smile at the very great consequence of his exploit in the lady's eyes, " if I was a-goin' to start out to save people's lives generally I wouldn't have thought a case o' whoopin' cough would be of much use savin' a man from drownin', and I'm sure if a feller fell out of a balloon it wouldn't help him much if he had ninety dozen cases o' whoopin' cough concealed on his person; but for just so long as I'm the feller that has to come up here every June, an' shoo the bears out o' the hotel, I ain't never goin' to be without a spell of whoopin' cough along about that time if I can help it. I wouldn't have been here now if it hadn't been for it."

" You referred just now," said Sapphira, " to shooing bears out of the hotel. May I inquire what useful function in the ménage of a hotel a bear-shooer performs? "

" What useful what? " asked Beelzy.

" Function—duty—what does the duty of a bear-shooer consist in? " explained Mr. Munchausen. " Is he a blacksmith who shoes bears instead of horses? "

" He's a bear-chaser," explained Beelzy, " and I'm it," he added. " That, Ma'am, is the function of a bear-shoer in the menagerie of a hotel."

Sapphira having expressed herself as satisfied, Beelzebub continued.

" You see this here house is shut up all winter, and when everybody's gone and left it empty the bears come down out of the mountains and use it instead of a cave. It's more cosier and less windier than their dens. So when the last guest has gone, and all the doors are locked, and the band gone into winter quarters, down come the bears and take possession. They generally climb through some open window somewhere. They divide up all the best rooms accordin' to their position in bear society and settle down to a regular hotel life among themselves."

" But what do they feed upon? " asked Sapphira.

" Oh they'll eat anything when they're hungry," said Beelzy. " Sofa cushions, parlor rugs, hotel registers—anything they can fasten their teeth to. Last year they came in through the cupola, burrowin' down through the snow to get at it, and there they stayed enjoyin' life out o' reach o' the wind and storm, snug's bugs in rugs. Year before last there must ha' been a hundred of 'em in the hotel when I got here, but one by one I got rid of 'em. Some I smoked out with some cigars Mr. Munchausen gave me the summer before; some I deceived out, gettin' 'em to chase me through the winders, an' then doublin' back on my tracks an' lockin' 'em out. It was mighty wearin' work.

" Last June there was twice as many. By actual tab I shooed two hundred and eight bears and a panther off into the mountains. When the last one as I thought disappeared into the woods I searched the house from top to bottom to see if there was any more to be got rid of. Every blessed one of the five hundred rooms I went through, and not a bear was left that I could see. I can tell you, I was glad, because there was a partickerly ugly run of 'em this year, an' they gave me a pile o' trouble. They hadn't found much to eat in the hotel, an' they was disappointed and cross. As a matter of

138

fact, the only things they found in the place they could eat was a piano stool and an old hair trunk full o' paper-covered novels, which don't make a very hearty meal for two hundred and eight bears and a panther."

"I should say not," said Sapphira, "particularly if the novels were as light as most of them are nowadays."

"I can't say as to that," said Beelzy. "I ain't got time to read 'em and so I ain't any judge. But all this time I was sufferin' like hookey with awful spasms of whoopin' cough. I whooped so hard once it smashed one o' the best echoes in the place all to flinders, an' of course that made the work twice as harder. So, naturally, when I found there warn't another bear left in the hotel, I just threw myself down anywhere, and slept. My! how I slept. I don't suppose anything ever slept sounder'n I did. And then it happened."

Beelzy gave his trousers a hitch and let his voice drop to a stage whisper that lent a wondrous impressiveness to his narration.

139

"As I was a-layin' there unconscious, dreamin' of home and father, a great big black hungry bruin weighin' six hundred and forty-three pounds, that had been hidin' in the bread oven in the bakery, where I hadn't thought of lookin' for him, came saunterin' along, hummin' a little tune all by himself, and lickin' his chops with delight at the idee of havin' me raw for his dinner. I lay on unconscious of my danger, until he got right up close, an' then I waked up, an' openin' my eyes saw this great black savage thing gloatin' over me an' tears of joy runnin' out of his mouth as he thought of the choice meal he was about to have. He was sniffin' my bang when I first caught sight of him."

"Mercy!" cried Sapphira, "I should think you'd have died of fright."

"I did," said Beelzy, politely, "but I came to life again in a minute. 'Oh Lor!' says I, as I see how hungry he was. 'This here's the end o' me;' at which the bear looked me straight in the eye, licked his chops again, and was about to take a nibble off my right ear when 'Whoop!' I had a spasm of

140

"At the first whoop Mr. Bear jumped ten
feet and fell over backwards on the floor."
Chapter XII.

whoopin'. Well, Ma'am, I guess you know what that means. There ain't nothin' more uncanny, more terrifyin' in the whole run o' human noises, barrin' a German Opery, than the whoop o' the whoopin' cough. At the first whoop Mr. Bear jumped ten feet and fell over backwards onto the floor; at the second he scrambled to his feet and put for the door, but stopped and looked around hopin' he was mistaken, when I whooped a third time. The third did the business. That third whoop would have scared Indians. It was awful. It was like a tornado blowin' through a fog-horn with a megaphone in front of it. When he heard that, Mr. Bear turned on all four of his heels and started on a scoot up into the woods that must have carried him ten miles before I quit coughin'.

" An' that's why, Ma'am, I say that when you've got to shoo bears for a livin', an attack o' whoopin' cough is a useful thing to have around."

Saying which, Beelzy departed to find Number 433's left boot which he had left at Number 334's door by some odd mistake.

"What do you think of that, Mr. Munchausen?" asked Sapphira, as Beelzy left the room.

"I don't know," said Mr. Munchausen, with a sigh. "I'm inclined to think that I am a trifle envious of him. The rest of us are not in his class."

XIII

IT was in the afternoon of a beautiful summer day, and Mr. Munchausen had come up from the simmering city of Cimmeria to spend a day or two with Diavolo and Angelica and their venerable parents. They had all had dinner, and were now out on the back piazza overlooking the magnificent river Styx, which flowed from the mountains to the sea, condescending on its way thither to look in upon countless insignificant towns which had grown up on its banks, among which was the one in which Diavolo and Angelica had been born and lived all their lives. Mr. Munchausen was lying comfortably in a hammock, collecting his thoughts.

Angelica was somewhat depressed, but Diavolo was jubilant and all because in the course of a walk they had had that morning Diavolo had killed a snake.

"It was fine sport," said Diavolo. "He was lying there in the sun, and I took a stick and put him out of his misery in two minutes."

143

Here Diavolo illustrated the process by whacking the Baron over his waist-coat with a small malacca stick he carried.

" Well, I didn't like it," said Angelica. " I don't care for snakes, but somehow or other it seems to me we'd ought to have left him alone. He wasn't hurting anybody off there. If he'd come walking on our place, that would have been one thing, but we went walking where he was, and he had as much right to take a sun-bath there as we had."

" That's true enough," put in Mr. Munchausen, resolved after Diavolo's whack, to side against him. " You've just about hit it, Angelica. It wasn't polite of you in the first place, to disturb his snake-ship in his nap, and having done so, I can't see why Diavolo wanted to kill him."

" Oh, pshaw ! " said Diavolo, airily. " What's snakes good for except to kill? I'll kill 'em every chance I get. They aren't any good."

" All right," said Mr. Munchausen, quietly. " I suppose you know all about it; but I know a thing or two about snakes myself that do not exactly agree with what you say. They are some good sometimes, and, as a matter of fact, as a general rule, they are less apt to attack you without reason than you are to attack them. A snake is rather inclined to mind its own business unless he finds it necessary to do otherwise. Occasionally too you'll find a snake with a truly amiable character. I'll never forget my old pet Wriggletto, for instance, and as long as I remember him I can't help having a warm corner for snakes in my heart."

Here Mr. Munchausen paused and puffed thoughtfully on his cigar as a far-away half-affectionate look came into his eye.

"Who was Wriggletto?" asked Diavolo, transferring a half dollar from Mr. Munchausen's pocket to his own.

"Who was he?" cried Mr. Munchausen. "You don't mean to say that I have never told you about Wriggletto, my pet boa-constrictor, do you?"

"You never told me," said Angelica. "But I'm not everybody. Maybe you've told some other little Imps."

"No, indeed!" said Mr. Munchausen. "You two are the only little Imps I tell stories to, and as

145

far as I am concerned, while I admit you are not everybody you are somebody and that's more than everybody is. Wriggletto was a boa-constrictor I once knew in South America, and he was without exception, the most remarkable bit of a serpent I ever met. Genial, kind, intelligent, grateful and useful, and, after I'd had him a year or two, wonderfully well educated. He could write with himself as well as you or I can with a pen. There's a recommendation for you. Few men are all that—and few boa-constrictors either, as far as that goes. I admit Wriggletto was an exception to the general run of serpents, but he was all that I claim for him, nevertheless."

" What kind of a snake did you say he was? " asked Diavolo.

" A boa-constrictor," said Mr. Munchausen, " and I knew him from his childhood. I first encountered Wriggletto about ten miles out of Para on the river Amazon. He was being swallowed by a larger boa-constrictor, and I saved his life by catching hold of his tail and pulling him out just as the other was getting ready to give the last gulp which would have taken Wriggletto in completely, and placed him beyond all hope of ever being saved."

"What was the other boa doing while you were saving Wriggletto?" asked Diavolo, who was fond always of hearing both sides to every question, and whose father, therefore, hoped he might some day grow up to be a great judge, or at least serve with distinction upon a jury.

"He couldn't do anything," returned Mr. Munchausen. "He was powerless as long as Wriggletto's head stuck in his throat and just before I got the smaller snake extracted I killed the other one by cutting off his tail behind his ears. It was not a very dangerous rescue on my part as long as Wriggletto was likely to be grateful. I must confess for a minute I was afraid he might not comprehend all I had done for him, and it was just possible he might attack me, but the hug he gave me when he found himself free once more was reassuring. He wound himself gracefully around my body, squeezed me gently and then slid off into the road again, as much as to say 'Thank you, sir.

147

you're a brick.' After that there was nothing Wrigg-letto would not do for me. He followed me every-where I went from that time on. He seemed to learn all in an instant that there were hundreds of little things to be done about the house of an old bachelor like myself which a willing serpent could do, and he made it his business to do those things: like picking up my collars from the floor, and find-ing my studs for me when they rolled under the bureau, and a thousand and one other little serv-ices of a like nature, and when you, Master Diav-olo, try in future to say that snakes are only good to kill and are of no use to any one, you must at least make an exception in favour of Wriggletto."

"I will," said Diavolo, "But you haven't told us of the other useful things he did for you yet."

"I was about to do so," said Mr. Munchausen. "In the first place, before he learned how to do lit-tle things about the house for me, Wriggletto acted as a watch-dog and you may be sure that nobody ever ventured to prowl around my house at night while Wriggletto slept out on the lawn. Para was quite full of conscienceless fellows, too, at that time, any one of whom would have been glad to have a chance to relieve me of my belongings if they could get by my watch-snake. Two of them tried it one dark stormy night, and Wriggletto when he discovered them climbing in at my window, crawled up behind them and winding his tail about them crept down to the banks of the Amazon, dragging them after him. There he tossed them into the river, and came back to his post once more."

"Did you see him do it, Uncle Munch?" asked Angelica.

"No, I did not. I learned of it afterwards. Wriggletto himself said never a word. He was too modest for that," said Mr. Munchausen. "One of the robbers wrote a letter to the Para newspapers about it, complaining that any one should be allowed to keep a reptile like that around, and suggested that anyhow people using snakes in place of dogs should be compelled to license them, and put up a sign at their gates:

> # BEWARE OF THE SNAKE!

"The man never acknowledged, of course, that he was the robber,—said that he was calling on business when the thing happened,—but he didn't say what his business was, but I knew better, and later on the other robber and he fell out, and they confessed that the business they had come on was to take away a few thousand gold coins of the realm which I was known to have in the house locked in a steel chest.

"I bought Wriggletto a handsome silver collar after that, and it was generally understood that he was the guardian of my place, and robbers bothered me no more. Then he was finer than a cat for rats. On very hot days he would go off into the cellar, where it was cool, and lie there with his mouth wide open and his eyes shut, and catch rats by the dozens. They'd run around in the dark, and the first thing they'd know they'd stumble into Wriggletto's mouth; and he swallowed them and licked his chops afterwards, just as you or I do when we've swallowed a fine luscious oyster or a clam.

"But pleasantest of all the things Wriggletto

did for me—and he was untiring in his attentions in that way—was keeping me cool on hot summer nights. Para as you may have heard is a pretty hot place at best, lying in a tropical region as it does, but sometimes it is awful for a man used to the Northern climate, as I was. The act of fanning one's self, so far from cooling one off, makes one hotter than ever. Maybe you remember how it was with the elephant in the poem:

> "'Oh my, oh dear!' the elephant said,
>   'It is so awful hot!
> I've fanned myself for seventy weeks,
>   And haven't cooled a jot.'

"And that was the way it was with me in Para on hot nights. I'd fan and fan and fan, but I couldn't get cool until Wriggletto became a member of my family, and then I was all right. He used to wind his tail about a huge palm-leaf fan I had cut in the forest, so large that I couldn't possibly handle it myself, and he'd wave it to and fro by the hour, with the result that my house was always the breeziest place in Para."

151

"Where is Wriggletto now?" asked Diavolo.

"Heigho!" sighed Mr. Munchausen. "He died, poor fellow, and all because of that silver collar I gave him. He tried to swallow a jibola that entered my house one night on wickedness intent, and while Wriggletto's throat was large enough when he stretched it to take down three jibolas, with a collar on which wouldn't stretch he couldn't swallow one. He didn't know that, unfortunately, and he kept on trying until the jibola got a quarter way down and then he stuck. Each swallow, of course, made the collar fit more tightly and finally poor Wriggletto choked himself to death. I felt so badly about it that I left Para within a month, but meanwhile I had a suit of clothes made out of Wriggletto's skin, and wore it for years, and then, when the clothes began to look worn, I had the skin re-tanned and made over into shoes and slippers. So you see that even after death he was useful to me. He was a faithful snake, and that is why when I hear people running down all snakes I tell the story of Wriggletto."

"He used to wind his tail about a fan and he'd wave it to and fro by the hour."

Chapter XIII.

There was a pause for a few moments, when Diavolo said, " Uncle Munch, is that a true story you've been giving us? "

" True? " cried Mr. Munchausen. " True? Why, my dear boy, what a question! If you don't believe it, bring me your atlas, and I'll show you just where Para is."

Diavolo did as he was told, and sure enough, Mr. Munchausen did exactly as he said he would, which Diavolo thought was very remarkable, but he still was not satisfied.

" You said he could write as well with himself as you or I could with a pen, Uncle Munch," he said. " How was that? "

" Why that was simple enough," explained Mr. Munchausen. " You see he was very black, and thirty-nine feet long and remarkably supple and slender. After a year of hard study he learned to bunch himself into letters, and if he wanted to say anything to me he'd simply form himself into a written sentence. Indeed his favourite attitude when in repose showed his wonderful gift in chirog-

153

raphy as well as his affection for me. If you will get me a card I will prove it."

Diavolo brought Mr. Munchausen the card and upon it he drew the following:

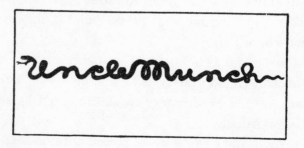

"There," said Mr. Munchausen. "That's the way Wriggletto always used to lie when he was at rest. His love for me was very affecting."

XIV

THE POETIC JUNE-BUG, TOGETHER WITH SOME RE-
MARKS ON THE GILLYHOOLY BIRD

"UNCLE MUNCH," said Diavolo one afternoon as a couple of bicyclers sped past
the house at breakneck speed, " which would you
rather have, a bicycle or a horse? "

"Well, I must say, my boy, that is a difficult
question to answer," Mr. Munchausen replied
after scratching his head dubiously for a few minutes. " You might as well ask a man which he
prefers, a hammock or a steam-yacht. To that
question I should reply that if I wanted to sell
it, I'd rather have a steam-yacht, but for a pleasant
swing on a cool piazza in midsummer or under the
apple-trees, a hammock would be far preferable.
Steam-yachts are not much good to swing in under
an apple tree, and very few piazzas that I know
of are big enough—"

"Oh, now, you know what I mean, Uncle
Munch," Diavolo retorted, tapping Mr. Munchau-

sen upon the end of his nose, for a twinkle in Mr. Munchausen's eye seemed to indicate that he was in one of his chaffing moods, and a greater tease than Mr. Munchausen when he felt that way no one has ever known. " I mean for horse-back riding, which would you rather have? "

" Ah, that's another matter," returned Mr. Munchausen, calmly. " Now I know how to answer your question. For horse-back riding I certainly prefer a horse; though, on the other hand, for bicycling, bicycles are better than horses. Horses make very poor bicycles, due no doubt to the fact that they have no wheels."

Diavolo began to grow desperate.

" Of course," Mr. Munchausen went on, " all I have to say in this connection is based merely on my ideas, and not upon any personal experience. I've been horse-back riding on horses, and bicycling on bicycles, but I never went horse-back riding on a bicycle, or bicycling on horseback. I should think it might be exciting to go bicycling on horse-back, but very dangerous. It is hard enough for me to keep a bicycle from toppling over when I'm riding on a hard, straight, level well-paved road, without experimenting with my wheel on a horse's back. However if you wish to try it some day and will get me a horse with a back as big as Trafalgar Square I'm willing to make the effort."

Angelica giggled. It was lots of fun for her when Mr. Munchausen teased Diavolo, though she didn't like it quite so much when it was her turn to be treated that way. Diavolo wanted to laugh too, but he had too much dignity for that, and to conceal his desire to grin from Mr. Munchausen he began to hunt about for an old newspaper, or a lump of coal or something else he could make a ball of to throw at him.

"Which would you rather do, Angelica," Mr. Munchausen resumed, "go to sea in a balloon or attend a dumb-crambo party in a chicken-coop?"

"I guess I would," laughed Angelica.

"That's a good answer," Mr. Munchausen put in. "It is quite as intelligent as the one which is attributed to the Gillyhooly bird. When the Gillyhooly bird was asked his opinion of giraffes, he scratched his head for a minute and said,

157

" ' The question hath but little wit
  That you have put to me,
But I will try to answer it
  With prompt candidity.

The automobile is a thing
  That's pleasing to the mind ;
And in a lustrous diamond ring
  Some merit I can find.

Some persons gloat o'er French Chateaux ;
  Some dote on lemon ice ;
While others gorge on mixed gateaux,
  Yet have no use for mice.

I'm very fond of oyster-stew,
  I love a patent-leather boot,
But after all, 'twixt me and you,
  The fish-ball is my favourite fruit.' "

" Hoh " jeered Diavolo, who, attracted by the allusion to a kind of bird of which he had never heard before, had given up the quest for a paper ball and returned to Mr. Munchausen's side, " I don't think that was a very intelligent answer. It didn't answer the question at all."

" That's true, and that is why it was intelligent," said Mr. Munchausen. " It was noncommittal. Some day when you are older and know less than you do now, you will realise, my dear

Diavolo, how valuable a thing is the reply that answereth not."

Mr. Munchausen paused long enough to let the lesson sink in and then he resumed.

"The Gillyhooly bird is a perfect owl for wisdom of that sort," he said. "It never lets anybody know what it thinks; it never makes promises, and rarely speaks except to mystify people. It probably has just as decided an opinion concerning giraffes as you or I have, but it never lets anybody into the secret."

"What is a Gillyhooly bird, anyhow?" asked Diavolo.

"He's a bird that never sings for fear of straining his voice; never flies for fear of wearying his wings; never eats for fear of spoiling his digestion; never stands up for fear of bandying his legs and never lies down for fear of injuring his spine," said Mr. Munchausen. "He has no feathers, because, as he says, if he had, people would pull them out to trim hats with, which would be painful, and he never goes into debt because, as he observes himself, he has no hope of paying the

159

bill with which nature has endowed him, so why run up others?"

"I shouldn't think he'd live long if he doesn't eat?" suggested Angelica.

"That's the great trouble," said Mr. Munchausen. "He doesn't live long. Nothing so ineffably wise as the Gillyhooly bird ever does live long. I don't believe a Gillyhooly bird ever lived more than a day, and that, connected with the fact that he is very ugly and keeps himself out of sight, is possibly why no one has ever seen one. He is known only by hearsay, and as a matter of fact, besides ourselves, I doubt if any one has ever heard of him."

Diavolo eyed Mr. Munchausen narrowly.

"Speaking of Gillyhooly birds, however, and to be serious for a moment," Mr. Munchausen continued flinching nervously under Diavolo's unyielding gaze; "I never told you about the poetic June-bug that worked the typewriter, did I?"

"Never heard of such a thing," cried Diavolo. "The idea of a June-bug working a typewriter."

160

"I don't believe it," said Angelica, "he hasn't got any fingers."

"That shows all you know about it," retorted Mr. Munchausen. "You think because you are half-way right you are all right. However, if you don't want to hear the story of the June-bug that worked the type-writer, I won't tell it. My tongue is tired, anyhow."

"Please go on," said Diavolo. "I want to hear it."

"So do I," said Angelica. "There are lots of stories I don't believe that I like to hear—'Jack the Giant-killer' and 'Cinderella,' for instance."

"Very well," said Mr. Munchausen. "I'll tell it, and you can believe it or not, as you please. It was only two summers ago that the thing happened, and I think it was very curious. As you may know, I often have a great lot of writing to do and sometimes I get very tired holding a pen in my hand. When you get old enough to write real long letters you'll know what I mean. Your writing hand will get so tired that sometimes you'll wish some wizard would come along smart enough to invent a machine by means of which everything you think can be transferred to paper as you think it, without the necessity of writing. But as yet the only relief to the man whose hand is worn out by the amount of writing he has to do is the use of the type-writer, which is hard only on the fingers. So to help me in my work two summers ago I bought a type-writing machine, and put it in the great bay-window of my room at the hotel where I was stopping. It was a magnificent hotel, but it had one drawback—it was infested with June-bugs. Most summer hotels are afflicted with mos-quitoes, but this one had June-bugs instead, and all night long they'd buzz and butt their heads against the walls until the guests went almost crazy with the noise.

" At first I did not mind it very much. It was amusing to watch them, and my friends and I used to play a sort of game of chance with them that entertained us hugely. We marked the walls off in squares which we numbered and then made little wagers as to which of the squares a spe-

162

cially selected June-bug would whack next. To simplify the game we caught the chosen June-bug and put some powdered charcoal on his head, so that when he butted up against the white wall he would leave a black mark in the space he hit. It was really one of the most exciting games of that particular kind that I ever played, and many a rainy day was made pleasant by this diversion.

" But after awhile like everything else June-bug Roulette as we called it began to pall and I grew tired of it and wished there never had been such a thing as a June-bug in the world. I did my best to forget them, but it was impossible. Their buzzing and butting continued uninterrupted, and toward the end of the month they developed a particularly bad habit of butting the electric call button at the side of my bed. The consequence was that at all hours of the night, hall-boys with iced-water, and house-maids with bath towels, and porters with kindling-wood would come knocking at my door and routing me out of bed—summoned of course by none other than those horrible butting insects. This particular nuisance became so unendurable that I had to change my room for one which had no electric bell in it.

"So things went, until June passed and July appeared. The majority of the nuisances promptly got out but one especially vigorous and athletic member of the tribe remained. He became unbearable and finally one night I jumped out of bed either to kill him or to drive him out of my apartment forever, but he wouldn't go, and try as I might I couldn't hit him hard enough to kill him. In sheer desperation I took the cover of my typewriting machine and tried to catch him in that. Finally I succeeded, and, as I thought, shook the heedless creature out of the window promptly slamming the window shut so that he might not return; and then putting the type-writer cover back over the machine, I went to bed again, but not to sleep as I had hoped. All night long every second or two I'd hear the type-writer click. This I attributed to nervousness on my part. As far as I knew there wasn't anything to make the type-writer click, and the fact that I heard it do so

"Most singular of all was the fact that consciously or unconsciously the insect had butted out a verse."

Chapter XIV.

served only to convince me that I was tired and imagined that I heard noises.

" The next morning, however, on opening the machine I found that the June-bug had not only not been shaken out of the window, but had actually spent the night inside of the cover, butting his head against the keys, having no wall to butt with it, and most singular of all was the fact that, consciously or unconsciously, the insect had butted out a verse which read :

> " ' I'm glad I haven't any brains,
> For there can be no doubt
> I'd have to give up butting
> If I had, or butt them out ' "

" Mercy! Really? " cried Angelica.

" Well I can't prove it," said Mr. Munchausen, " by producing the June-bug, but I can show you the hotel, I can tell you the number of the room ; I can show you the type-writing machine, and I have recited the verse. If you're not satisfied with that I'll have to stand your suspicions."

"What became of the June-bug?" demanded Diavolo.

"He flew off as soon as I lifted the top of the machine," said Mr. Munchausen. "He had all the modesty of a true poet and did not wish to be around while his poem was being read."

"It's queer how you can't get rid of June-bugs, isn't it, Uncle Munch," suggested Angelica.

"Oh, we got rid of 'em next season all right," said Mr. Munchausen. "I invented a scheme that kept them away all the following summer. I got the landlord to hang calendars all over the house with one full page for each month. Then in every room we exposed the page for May and left it that way all summer. When the June-bugs arrived and saw these, they were fooled into believing that June hadn't come yet, and off they flew to wait. They are very inconsiderate of other people's comfort," Mr. Munchausen concluded, "but they are rigorously bound by an etiquette of their own. A self-respecting June-bug would no more appear until the June-bug season is regularly open than a gentleman of high society would go to a five o'clock tea munching fresh-roasted peanuts. And by the way, that reminds me I happen to have a bag of peanuts right here in my pocket."

Here Mr. Munchausen, transferring the luscious goobers to Angelica, suddenly remembered that he had something to say to the Imps' father, and hurriedly left them.

"Do you suppose that's true, Diavolo?" whispered Angelica as their friend disappeared.

"Well it might happen," said Diavolo, "but I've a sort of notion that it's 'maginary like the Gillyhooly bird. Gimme a peanut."

XV

A LUCKY STROKE

"MR. MUNCHAUSEN," said Ananias, as he and the famous warrior drove off from the first hole at the Missing Links, "you never seem to weary of the game of golf. What is its precise charm in your eyes,—the health-giving qualities of the game or its capacity for bad lies?"

"I owe my life to it," replied the Baron. "That is to say to my precision as a player I owe one of the many preservations of my existence which have passed into history. Furthermore it is ever varying in its interest. Like life itself it is full of hazards and no man knows at the beginning of his stroke what will be the requirements of the next. I never told you of the bovine lie I got once while playing a match with Bonaparte, did I?"

"I do not recall it," said Ananias, foozling his second stroke into the stone wall.

"I was playing with my friend Bonaparte, for the Cosmopolitan Championship," said Munchausen, "and we were all even at the thirty-sixth hole.

A LUCKY STROKE

Bonaparte had sliced his ball into a stubble field from the tee, whereat he was inclined to swear, until by an odd mischance I drove mine into the throat of a bull that was pasturing on the fair green two hundred and ninety-eight yards distant. 'Shall we take it over?' I asked. 'No,' laughed Bonaparte, thinking he had me. 'We must play the game. I shall play my lie. You must play yours.' 'Very well,' said I. 'So be it. Golf is golf, bull or no bull.' And off we went. It took Bonaparte seven strokes to get on the green again, which left me a like number to extricate my ball from the throat of the unwelcome bovine. It was a difficult business, but I made short work of it. Tying my red silk handkerchief to the end of my brassey I stepped in front of the great creature and addressing an imaginary ball before him made the usual swing back and through stroke. The bull, angered by the fluttering red handkerchief, reared up and made a dash at me. I ran in the direction of the hole, the bull in pursuit for two hundred yards. Here I hid behind a tree while Mr. Bull stopped short and snorted again. Still there was no sign of the ball, and after my pursuer had quieted a little I emerged from my hiding place and with the same club and in the same manner played three. The bull surprised at my temerity threw his head back with an angry toss and tried to bellow forth his wrath, as I had designed he should, but the obstruction in his throat prevented him. The ball had stuck in his pharynx. Nothing came of his spasm but a short hacking cough and a wheeze—then silence. ' I'll play four,' I cried to Bonaparte, who stood watching me from a place of safety on the other side of the stone wall. Again I swung my red-flagged brassey in front of the angry creature's face and what I had hoped for followed. The second attempt at a bellow again resulted in a hacking cough and a sneeze, and lo the ball flew out of his throat and landed dead to the hole. The caddies drove the bull away. Bonaparte played eight, missed a putt for a nine, stymied himself in a ten, holed out in twelve and I went down in five."

" Jerusalem ! " cried Ananias. " What did Bonaparte say? "

" Again I swung my red-flagged brassey in
front of the angry creature's face, and what I
had hoped for followed."

Chapter XV.

"He delivered a short, quick nervous address in Corsican and retired to the club-house where he spent the afternoon drowning his sorrows in Absinthe high-balls. 'Great hole that, Bonaparte,' said I when his geniality was about to return. 'Yes,' said he. 'A regular lu-lu, eh?' said I. 'More than that, Baron,' said he. 'It was a Waterlooloo.' It was the first pun I ever heard the Emperor make."

"We all have our weak moments," said Ananias drily, playing nine from behind the wall. "I give the hole up," he added angrily.

"Let's play it out anyhow," said Munchausen, playing three to the green.

"All right," Ananias agreed, taking a ten and rimming the cup.

Munchausen took three to go down, scoring six in all.

"Two up," said he, as Ananias putted out in eleven.

"How the deuce do you make that out? This is only the first hole," cried Ananias with some show of heat.

"You gave up a hole, didn't you?" demanded Munchausen.

"Yes."

"And I won a hole, didn't I?"

"You did—but—"

"Well that's two holes. Fore!" cried Munchausen.

The two walked along in silence for a few minutes, and the Baron resumed.

"Yes, golf is a splendid game and I love it, though I don't think I'd ever let a good canvasback duck get cold while I was talking about it. When I have a canvasback duck before me I don't think of anything else while it's there. But unquestionably I'm fond of golf, and I have a very good reason to be. It has done a great deal for me, and as I have already told you, once it really saved my life."

"Saved your life, eh?" said Ananias.

"That's what I said," returned Mr. Munchausen, "and so of course that is the way it was."

"I should admire to hear the details," said An-

anias. " I presume you were going into a decline
and it restored your strength and vitality."

" No," said Mr. Munchausen, " it wasn't that
way at all.   It saved my life when I was attacked
by a fierce and ravenously hungry lion.   If I hadn't
known how to play golf it would have been farewell forever to Mr. Munchausen, and Mr. Lion
would have had a fine luncheon that day, at which
I should have been the turkey and cranberry sauce
and mince pie all rolled into one."

Ananias laughed.

" It's easy enough to laugh at my peril now,"
said Mr. Munchausen, " but if you'd been with me
you wouldn't have laughed very much.   On the
contrary, Ananias, you'd have ruined what little
voice you ever had screeching."

" I wasn't laughing at the danger you were in,"
said Ananias.   " I don't see anything funny in
that.   What I was laughing at was the idea of a
lion turning up on a golf course.   They don't have
lions on any of the golf courses that I am familiar
with."

" That may be, my dear Ananias," said Mr. Munchausen, " but it doesn't prove anything. What you are familiar with has no especial bearing upon the ordering of the Universe. They had lions by the hundreds on the particular links I refer to. I laid the links out myself and I fancy I know what I am talking about. They were in the desert of Sahara. And I tell you what it is," he added, slapping his knee enthusiastically, " they were the finest links I ever played on. There wasn't a hole shorter than three miles and a quarter, which gives you plenty of elbow room, and the fair green had all the qualities of a first class billiard table, so that your ball got a magnificent roll on it."

" What did you do for hazards? " asked Ananias.

" Oh we had 'em by the dozen," replied Mr. Munchausen. " There weren't any ponds or stone walls, of course, but there were plenty of others that were quite as interesting. There was the Sphynx for instance; and for bunkers the pyramids can't be beaten. Then occasionally right in the middle of a game a caravan ten or twelve miles long, would begin to drag its interminable length across the middle of the course, and it takes mighty nice work with the lofting iron to lift a ball over a caravan without hitting a camel or killing an Arab, I can tell you. Then finally I'm sure I don't know of any more hazardous hazard for a golf player— or for anybody else for that matter—than a real hungry African lion out in search of breakfast, especially when you meet him on the hole furthest from home and have a stretch of three or four miles between him and assistance with no revolver or other weapon at hand. That's hazard enough for me and it took the best work I could do with my brassey to get around it."

"You always were strong at a brassey lie," said Ananias.

"Thank you," said Mr. Munchausen. "There are few lies I can't get around. But on this morning I was playing for the Mid-African Championship. I'd been getting along splendidly. My record for fifteen holes was about seven hundred and eighty-three strokes, and I was flattering myself that I was about to turn in the best card that had ever been seen in a medal play contest in all

Africa. My drive from the sixteenth tee was a simple beauty. I thought the ball would never stop, I hit it such a tremendous whack. It had a flight of three hundred and eighty-two yards and a roll of one hundred and twenty more, and when it finally stopped it turned up in a mighty good lie on a natural tee, which the wind had swirled up. Calling to the monkey who acted as my caddy— we used monkeys for caddies always in Africa, and they were a great success because they don't talk and they use their tails as a sort of extra hand,—I got out my brassey for the second stroke, took my stance on the hardened sand, swung my club back, fixed my eye on the ball and was just about to carry through, when I heard a sound which sent my heart into my boots, my caddy galloping back to the club house, and set my teeth chattering like a pair of castanets. It was unmistakable, that sound. When a hungry lion roars you know precisely what it is the moment you hear it, especially if you have heard it before. It doesn't sound a bit like the miauing of a cat; nor is it suggestive of the rumble of artillery in an adjacent street. There is no mistaking it for distant thunder, as some writers would have you believe. It has none of the gently mournful quality that characterises the soughing of the wind through the leafless branches of the autumnal forest, to which a poet might liken it; it is just a plain lion-roaring and nothing else, and when you hear it you know it. The man who mistakes it for distant thunder might just as well be struck by lightning there and then for all the chance he has to get away from it ultimately. The poet who confounds it with the gentle soughing breeze never lives to tell about it. He gets himself eaten up for his foolishness. It doesn't require a Daniel come to judgment to recognise a lion's roar on sight.

" I should have perished myself that morning if I had not known on the instant just what were the causes of the disturbance. My nerve did not desert me, however, frightened as I was. I stopped my play and looked out over the sand in the direction whence the roaring came, and there he stood a perfect picture of majesty, and a giant among lions, eyeing me critically as much as to say, ' Well this is luck, here's breakfast fit for a king!' but he reckoned without his host. I was in no mood to be served up to stop his ravening appetite and I made up my mind at once to stay and fight. I'm a good runner, Ananias, but I cannot beat a lion in a three mile sprint on a sandy soil, so fight it was. The question was how. My caddy gone, the only weapons I had with me were my brassey and that one little gutta percha ball, but thanks to my golf they were sufficient.

" Carefully calculating the distance at which the huge beast stood, I addressed the ball with unusual care, aiming slightly to the left to overcome my tendency to slice, and drove the ball straight through the lion's heart as he poised himself on his hind legs ready to spring upon me. It was a superb stroke and not an instant too soon, for just as the ball struck him he sprang forward, and even as it was landed but two feet away from where I stood, but, I am happy to say, dead.

" It was indeed a narrow escape, and it tried my nerves to the full, but I extracted the ball and resumed my play in a short while, adding the lucky stroke to my score meanwhile. But I lost the match,—not because I lost my nerve, for this I did not do, but because I lifted from the lion's heart. The committee disqualified me because I did not play from my lie and the cup went to my competitor. However, I was satisfied to have escaped with my life. I'd rather be a live runner-up than a dead champion any day."

"A wonderful experience," said Ananias. "Perfectly wonderful. I never heard of a stroke to equal that."

"You are too modest, Ananias," said Mr. Munchausen drily. "Too modest by half. You and Sapphira hold the record for that, you know."

"I have forgotten the episode," said Ananias.

"Didn't you and she make your last hole on a single stroke?" demanded Munchausen with an inward chuckle.

"Oh—yes," said Ananias grimly, as he recalled the incident. "But you know we didn't win any more than you did."

"Oh, didn't you?" asked Munchausen.

" No," replied Ananias. " You forget that Sapphira and I were two down at the finish."

And Mr. Munchausen played the rest of the game in silence. Ananias had at last got the best of him.

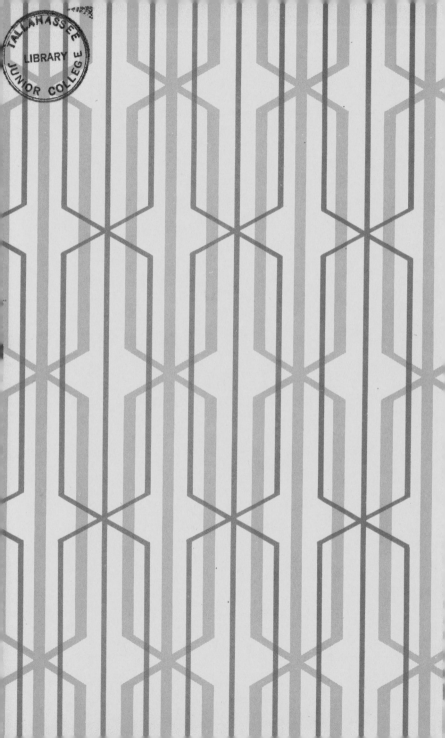